Praise fo

An emotional, complex and beautiful story of love and life and how it can all change in a heartbeat.

—DiDi, Guilty Pleasures Book Reviews on *Texas Lullaby*

Highly recommend to all fans of hot cowboys, firefighters, and romance.

—Emily, Goodreads on *Saddles and Soot*

This author does an amazing job of keeping readers on their toes while maintaining a natural flow to the story.

—RT Book Reviews on *Texas Hustle*

Cynthia D'Alba's *Texas Fandango* from Samhain lets readers enjoy the sensual fun in the sun [...] This latest offering gives readers a sexy escape and a reason to seek out D'Alba's earlier titles.

—Library Journal Reviews on *Texas Fandango*

[…] inclusions that stand out for all the right reasons is Cynthia D'Alba's clever *Backstage Pass*

—Publisher's Weekly on *Backstage Pass* in *Cowboy Heat*

Texas Two Step kept me on an emotional roller coaster […] an emotionally charged romance, with well-developed characters and an engaging secondary cast. A quarter of the way into the book I added Ms. D'Alba to my auto-buys.

—5 Stars and Recommended Read, Guilty Pleasure Book Reviews on *Texas Two Step*

[..]Loved this book…characters came alive. They had depth, interest and completeness. But more than the romance and sex which were great, there are connections with family and friends which makes this story so much more than a story about two people.

—Night Owl Romance 5 STARS! A TOP PICK *on Texas Bossa Nova*

Wow, what an amazing romance novel. *Texas Lullaby* is an impassioned, well-written book with a genuine love story that took hold of my heart and soul from the very beginning.

—LJT, Amazon Reviews, on *Texas Lullaby*

Texas Lullaby is a refreshing departure from the traditional romance plot in that it features an already committed couple.

—Tangled Hearts Book Reviews on *Texas Lullaby*

[…]sexy, contemporary western has it all. Scorching sex, a loving family and suspenseful danger. Oh, yeah!

—Bookaholics Romance Book Club on *Texas Hustle*

Also by Cynthia D'Alba

SADDLES AND SOOT

Whispering Springs, Texas

CYNTHIA D'ALBA

SADDLES AND SOOT

By Cynthia D'Alba

Copyright © 2015 Cynthia D'Alba and Riante, Inc.

Print ISBN: 978-0-9982650-2-5

Digital ISBN: 978-0-9982650-3-2

Cover Artists: Elle James

Editor: Carolyn Depew

Chapter One

Georgina Greyson used her toes to push her porch swing into a lazy sway as she sorted her mail. Today's bundle contained a mixture of unwanted advertising, store ads, and a couple of bills.

And then she came to the final envelope. Cream-colored, of heavy stock with fancy script writing, she was sure it could only be one thing…an invitation. Flipping it over to check the return address, she wasn't surprised. It was what she had expected. An invitation to her ex-fiancé's wedding.

She slid her nail under the flap and pulled out the heavy card with a swirling black font.

Priscilla Eileen Duvall
and
Christopher Joseph Lemon
Request the Pleasure
of Your Presence

Blah, blah, blah.

Yeah, yeah, Priscilla. You got him to marry you. Marriage won't be all you think it will.

The wedding had been last month. With all of the moving associated with her veterinary internship, the invitation had taken some time to catch up with Georgina through mail forwarding. But still, a month was a long time…. She checked the postmark. Had Priscilla actually mailed this after the ceremony to make sure Georgina knew her ex was off the market? Or maybe Priscilla wanted to make sure her groom showed up before she crowed.

As she'd suspected, the postmark was the day after the wedding.

Georgina chuckled to herself with a shake of her head. She'd dodged a bullet when Chris had dumped her for her best friend Priscilla. Too bad he'd waited until they were standing at the altar to do so. At the time, she hadn't thought herself lucky, positive her life was over, even if she survived the embarrassment. Today, a year later, she was thankful to have avoided what she was sure would have been a matrimonial error of epic proportions. She mentally wished them well and put the card with the rest of the trash to be burned.

Resting her head against the cedar plank back, Georgina pushed off again and set the swing in motion. Whispering Springs, Texas was exactly what she needed right now…a small community and a job guaranteed to keep her busy and her mind off her non-existent love life.

And speaking of her love life, it really was time to get rid of all the pictures and notes and other memorabilia from her years with Chris. Why she'd moved it around with her was a mystery even to her. Most likely it was related to her years in the foster system and her lack of ability to take much with her when she was rehoused from family to family. Now she had a problem letting go.

No more, she vowed as she stood. No time like the present to do a little housecleaning.

Her parents had died when she'd been only two years old, so she had no memories of them. She'd lived with her maternal grandmother until her death when Georgie had been ten. Living on a large farm, her grandmother always burned the trash, something Georgie had loved doing with her. Since then she'd lived in cities where burning her trash really wasn't an option, not without drawing the cops and fire department to her door. Then again, maybe a cute cop or fireman might have been the answer to her love life drought.

But Whispering Springs was different. She lived outside town on a small farm with just enough acreage to make her feel a little country. No crops to tend, but there was a horse, a cow and a goat to care for during her stay. That was part of the rental agreement, not that she minded. Along with the four barn cats, they gave her some company.

She found the box marked "Crap" in the spare

bedroom and hauled it outside to the blackened area ringed with rocks where she assumed previous tenants had burned their trash. Then she gathered up all the newspapers and junk mail that'd been accumulating over the past week. Might as well get rid of those while she was at it.

She found perverse pleasure as she watched the flames lick and then consume the wedding invitation. Fire cleansed, and after seeing the cream-color turn to black ash, she felt the relief of the past being lifted off her shoulders.

Speaking of shoulders, she remembered an old jacket that belonged to Chris in her closet. Heck, yeah. She'd burn that too. And maybe even that pair of running shoes he'd left at her house that'd somehow gotten packed and moved.

The fire burned low and Georgie hurried into the house to grab those items. While there, she found a couple of shirts and a pair of jeans of his that definitely needed to be torched. Collecting the wad of old Chris-clothing in her arms, she hot-footed it back to the now barely-burning fire and dropped everything on top.

Her phone buzzed. She wasn't technically on-call this weekend but she'd promised Dr. Mabee that she'd be around if an emergency came up. But when she saw the name on the readout, she smiled. Magda Hobbs Montgomery was the reason Georgie had ended up in Texas.

"Hey, girlfriend. What's shakin' bacon?"

Magda laughed. "Man, I haven't heard that in years."

Georgie returned the laugh. "No one but you would get it. Glad you called."

"You okay?"

"Oh, sure. Getting settled in nicely." Georgie went back to the porch swing and sat. "I'm glad I had a few days to get settled before I have to go to work."

"Where's Mabee going again?"

"Australia. Some research trip he's been dying to do, to hear him tell it. Personally, I think it's just an excuse for an extended second honeymoon."

"When do you actually start work?"

"Tomorrow. He's taking me around to meet all the ranchers and cattlemen so they'll know me if they need to call the clinic."

"Oh goodie. He'll bring you by here then. Try to make it about one and I'll have lunch for you both."

"You don't have to do that," Georgie protested.

"Honey, you know me. I don't do anything I don't want to."

Georgie laughed. "True."

"Plus I want you to meet Reno."

"Kind of taken with that husband of yours."

Magda sighed. "You have no idea."

The scent of smoke filtered around the side of the house. "I guess I'd better check on my fire."

"Your what?" Magda shouted. "Fire? Your house is on fire?"

"No, no. Nothing like that. I was burning trash,

and a few things that needed to be permanently disposed of."

"There's a burn ban on right now. County's as dry as I've ever seen it. You might want to go put that fire out pronto."

"Burn ban? Seriously? I didn't know. I'll—"

The sound of a siren interrupted her. "I hear a siren close by. Guess you're probably right about putting out the fire. Holler at you later."

The smoke rolling around from the back of the house was heavier and darker now. Probably those darn running shoes smoldering. Maybe she should have thrown those into a Salvation Army bin. Too late now.

She screwed the hose nozzle onto the faucet at the side of the house and dragged the hose around to douse the fire. The unexpected heat from the growing blaze pushed her back. Somehow the fire had jumped its rock boundary and was eating its way toward the house.

Crap, crap, crap.

She'd begun frantically spraying the hose when a large, red firetruck braked to a stop in front of her house. Three men in tan turnout coats and pants jumped from the truck and scrambled for equipment. Behind the fire engine, five trucks skidded to a stop, red strobe lights on the dashes flashing through the windshields.

"Grab the hose and let's get it around back," the tall man from the first pickup truck shouted. "Buddy, be sure to get the fitting tight this time. We need all the water we can get." He shoved past Georgie with a gruff, "Move, lady."

Two firemen raced past her dragging a large hose toward her fire. Good grief. It wasn't even that big of a fire. Sure, it'd gotten out of its assigned location but she could have handled it with a simple garden hose. What an overreaction. Typical small volunteer fire department.

As that thought crossed her mind, the pine tree close to her bedroom window crackled as fire leapt up into its branches.

The animals! She needed to make sure they were okay.

Whirling around, she raced around the front of the house and approached the shared pasture from the other side of the house. Surprisingly, she found three more firemen there putting out small fires that'd started in the dead grass in the yard.

Running past them, she got to the fence and saw all three animals watching the firemen with a mixture of curiosity and fear. None of the burn paths had led to the pasture, so none of the animals she'd been trusted to protect were at risk. Even the smoke wasn't as thick over here.

The volume of water the firemen's hose sprayed was much greater than anything she could have generated with her garden hose. Within fifteen minutes, the fire was out and the men were rolling up their hose to leave.

A pain in the patoot for sure, but no real harm done.

The tall man who'd rudely shoved her out of the way stalked toward her with long strides and heavy footsteps.

"Lady," he said, his face red with either heat exposure or anger.

Georgie crossed her fingers for heat exposure. She was wrong.

"Are you nuts or stupid?" the man shouted. "You don't look crazy, so I'm going with stupid. There's a fire ban right now. That means *no fires*. At all. For any reason." He jerked the helmet off his head. Dark wavy hair fell over his forehead. "Well?" he demanded. A pair of chocolate brown eyes glared at her.

"Well, what?"

"Are you crazy or stupid?"

Georgie cocked her fists on her hips and widened her stance, hoping she looked intimidating. Sometimes that worked with her patients. Not with this guy.

"I'm neither, thankyouverymuch. I just got into town. I didn't know about the burn ban. Sorry. It wasn't part of the orientation to my house." She waved her hand toward the white clapboard house, as if he wouldn't know which house she was talking about. "Besides, no real harm done. I'm sure I could have put it out with a garden hose."

The man was a good six inches taller than she, and he took advantage of that stature to lean over her. "You know how a big fire gets started? With a small one. Yours would have spread fast if someone hadn't seen the smoke rising and contacted us. And ignorance of the ban is no excuse. Any person with a modicum of intelligence would have noticed the parched grass and dying trees around them. Get some glasses, lady, if you can't see that."

Ire rumbled in her gut. Standing on her tiptoes, she poked her finger into his chest, which was akin to poking the butcher block countertop in the kitchen. Dadgum near broke her finger. "I'm not stupid. And I'm not blind. And I'm sorry." She dropped down off her toes. "Thank you for showing up. Am I going to get a fine?"

The corners of his mouth twitched as though he might smile, but the movement went no further. "That'll be up to Sheriff Singer, but he's a good guy. He might go easy on you if you explain." His sexy chestnut eyes squinted into a serious expression. "No matter where you live, *always* check with the fire department before you burn."

She stepped back and saluted. "Yes, sir."

That did produce a tiny smile. The man turned on his boot heel and headed back to the truck. With engines growling, all six vehicles roared back down her drive to the highway. There, they went in separate directions.

She'd never experienced a volunteer fire department response. Interesting would be one word to describe it.

And the head of the response? He'd be best described as intriguing.

TANNER MARSHALL REMOVED HIS TURNOUT PANTS and hung them in the back of his truck, along with the coat he'd already stowed. After tossing his helmet on the floorboard, he shut the rear door.

"Glad you were here, Tanner," Marcie Townsend said. "With the Chief in Virginia at that conference, we're a little short-handed in the leadership department."

Tanner grinned at Marcie. Fifty years old with blonde hair and the body of a twenty-year-old model, Marcie had been the heart and soul of the Whispering Springs South Volunteer Fire Department for over thirty years. "Marcie, honey, don't kid a kidder. Sam may have the title of chief, but you run this place."

"I know, but don't let Sam hear that. He's hard enough to live with as it is."

Tanner laughed. Sam and Marcie had been married since high school. Their seven kids were now grown and had joined the volunteer department as soon as each had hit eighteen. Those seven were now producing the next generation of volunteer firefighters, the oldest of whom was about five, he guessed.

"Must not have been much of a fire. Y'all got back fast enough."

"Nah. Not too bad but it was definitely on its way when we got there. Damn place butts right up to my family's. Lucky for us that Zack was actually out working our cattle this morning instead of being on another ranch."

"How is your brother?"

"Mean and feisty."

Marcie laughed. "He's young. Give him time."

"I will but it's hard. You know Dad and Mom left last week for her dream vacation?"

"Of course I know. Your mom drove the RV by here so I could see their home-away-from-home. You think they'll really be gone for six months?"

Tanner ran his fingers through his damp hair, the sweat making his scalp itch. "No clue. That's what they said, but we'll see."

"Your mom had no qualms about leaving you in charge. You'll do fine with the ranch."

"Ah, hell, woman. It's not the ranch I'll have trouble with. It's the twins. I'm sure they'll drive me to drinking before the year is out."

Tanner had three younger siblings. At twenty-five, Zack was the closest in age, even though there was a nine year difference. The twins, Dillon and Deborah, were in their final year of high school and, in his opinion, the term "senioritis" had been invented for them. Both of them were too smart for their own good.

"Well, call me if you need anything," Marcie said as she patted his head. Of course she had to stand on her tiptoes to reach his head. "I've raised one or two or seven high school seniors."

Tanner bent down and kissed her cheek. "Don't think I won't."

He turned to walk away when Marcie called after him, "You want me to notify Sheriff Singer to drop by and have a talk with today's firebug?"

He stopped, his back to the volunteer fire department's office manager slash secretary. In his mind, he saw riotous red curls framing a porcelain face with an upturn at the tip of the nose and vibrant jade-green eyes. Full pouty lips that had tightened into a frown, and then just as quickly, released into a smile formed by full pouty lips that just seemed to beg to be kissed.

Smiling to himself, he didn't turn around to answer Marcie. The woman had a radar for picking up the most subtle of vibes.

"No. I don't think so. I don't think it'll happen again."

"But you'll go by and talk with her yourself?"

Busted.

"I never said the fire was started by a woman." This time he did look over his shoulder.

Marcie wore a you-can't-fool-me-grin. She arched an eyebrow. "Seven sons, Tanner. I always know."

He laughed and, shaking his head, walked away.

TANNER PARKED HIS TRUCK NEAR THE BARN AND climbed out. The stalls needed to be picked and troughs rinsed out and filled with fresh water. A horse whinnied to him when he entered.

"Hey, girl. Be there in a minute."

A black head popped over the stall gate. She gave a loud snort in his direction.

"You poor, poor momma. Is junior kicking you today?"

He made his way down to Jolene's stall. The pregnant mare butted her head against his shoulder. He scratched behind her ears, her favorite spot.

"I know. It's hard being a woman."

As though agreeing with his sentiment, she nodded her head and then lowered it for more stroking. The pregnancy had gone well so far. Not that he would admit this to anyone, but dealing with a pregnant four-year-old mare made him nervous, especially given Jolene's dam history.

Heaven help him if he ever had to deal with a pregnant woman!

"Get the fire out?"

Tanner glanced toward the barn's opening. "Yup. Thanks for the shout."

Zack walked down the barn aisle to give Jolene a few strokes. "I knew when I saw the smoke from the old Perrone place that you needed to check it out. What happened?"

"A ditz with a passion for burning trash."

Zack rolled his eyes. "What a lamebrain."

"You said it." Tanner nuzzled his forehead against Jolene's face. "How do you think she's doing?"

"Jolene? Good, as far as I can tell. What'd Doc Mabee say the last time he was here?"

"That she was the picture of health, but it still makes me nervous."

"Well, she doesn't have much longer."

"Yeah, and I can't believe Mabee will be gone for the delivery."

"You met the new vet yet?"

"Nope. Mabee said he'd bring Dr. Greyson around to meet everyone before he leaves."

"Greyson got a first name?"

"George, I think." Tanner shook his head. "I could be wrong, but I'm pretty sure that's what Mabee called him."

"Mabee say anything about the guy?"

"Only that Dr. Greyson was an excellent vet and we'd probably not want him to come home from Australia."

Zack chuckled and then wrinkled his nose. "You smell like smoke."

"I know. I thought I'd muck the stalls and then take a shower."

"You'll get no argument from me," Zack said with a laugh. "Why don't I move her highness outside for some fresh air while you freshen her palace?"

Tanner chuckled. "I think Jolene would like that."

Mucking was one of those chores he didn't enjoy but it was a reality of ranch life. At thirty-four, he needed to make up his mind about his future. Flying Eagle Cattle Company belonged to his parents, and sure, he could stay here and work with them, but was that what he wanted? To stay under the successful wing of his parents?

Or was it time for him to discover his own path? And if it was, where did he start?

He loved the ranch work. Loved being outdoors all day. Loved being on horseback. Even loved the smell of fresh hay.

But he also loved the years he'd spent in the

Lexington City Fire Department in Lexington, Kentucky. With his experience and education, he'd been approached by the Whispering Springs City Fire Department about joining them on a full-time basis. But he'd come home a couple of years ago to help his parents with their growing cattle business, not take up firefighting again. Joining the city fire department would put him too far away from Flying Eagle to be much help on a daily basis.

He dumped a load of horse manure into the wheelbarrow as he continued to think. The pressure to make long-range plans weighed him down. He was a man who liked to know where he was going, when he was going and with whom.

He didn't have to make a life plan today. Until his parents return, he was stuck here, not that he minded all that much. It gave him time to study his options and maybe make a plan for the future.

One aspect of his future remained hazy…the wife component. He hadn't had a long-term girlfriend since his mid-twenties. Frankly, lately he had gotten bored with the whole dating scene. He was ready to settle down with one woman. Build a life. Have kids, dogs, a white picket fence. The whole shebang.

The image of a smiling petite, red-headed firebug with flashing green eyes poking him in his chest flashed into his mind.

He shook his head. Nope. Anyone but her.

Chapter Two

❦

Seven a.m. The twins were running behind schedule, as usual. Tanner cupped his hand around his mouth. "Move it, guys. You're going to be late for school."

"I'm coming," Deborah yelled down the stairs. "I can't find my red boots. Do you know where they are?"

"In my room," Dillon shouted. "You left them here last night when we were doing homework."

"Oh. Right. Thanks."

Tanner shook his head and went back to the kitchen for another cup of coffee. Wrangling teenagers had to be worse than wrangling cats. If nothing else, this experience was making him a true believer in birth control.

Birth control. Damn. Did he need to talk to the twins about that, or had his parents already covered the subject with them? He groaned and ran a hand down his face. He was too young to feel this old.

Maybe he needed to rethink his whole settling down with a wife and kids scenario.

Heavy pounding on the stairs announced the twins' arrival seconds before they hit the kitchen like a couple of category five tornados, swiping food off the table, grabbing books off the counter and running out the door with quick waves and a "See ya this after-noon." The door slammed behind them and a deafening quiet fell over the house.

Tanner rubbed his face again. He was never that loud and rowdy at seventeen, right?

The back door slammed again after admitting Zack. "Thank God the coffee's hot. We got anything for breakfast?" He dropped into a chair at the table.

"We did. Sausage and biscuits, but a herd of locusts went through and devoured the entire plate."

Zack laughed. "And that is why Mom always hid a few."

Tanner hitched a thumb over his shoulder. "In the oven. I wasn't keeping them safe as much as keeping them warm."

"Ah. You're a good bro." After loading a plate with seven biscuits stuffed with thick spicy sausage, Zack sat again.

"I was never like Dillon and Deb, right? I mean loud and rowdy, and always losing things."

Zack shrugged. "I don't remember. I was only 8 when you were a senior. I thought you were the coolest guy in the world, so anything you did was right by me."

"Awww. How sweet."

"Yeah, and then I grew up and found out you could be a prick."

Tanner laughed. "Backatcha, bro."

His brother swallowed and took a big slug of coffee. "What's on the agenda today?"

"Well, grocery shopping for sure. Did you get down to the barn yet this morning?"

"Only to let Jolene into the pasture. Poor girl. Her bulging sides make me hurt."

"So glad the men don't have to be the pregnant ones."

The two brothers clinked coffee mugs in agreement.

"So we have mucking and laundry to do this morning." Tanner blew out a breath. "How did our parents do all this when we were younger? I'm exhausted just trying to remember everything."

"Don't ask me. So you want to go to the store or want me to go?"

"Doc Mabee is bringing around the new vet today. I want to be here to meet him. Get a feel of how he is with the animals, you know? So it's the store for you, mucking and laundry for me. List is on the fridge."

Zack tilted his chair back on its rear legs until he could snatch the paper under the magnet, then he let the front legs bang back on the floor. He glanced down the paper. "Oh, hell no." Thrusting the list toward Tanner, he said, "You do this. I'll wait here for the vet."

Tanner frowned. "What?"

"I am not going into Whispering Springs and buying tampons for Deb."

Chuckling, Tanner scanned the items. Sure enough, their sister had added tampons, the brand, the number in the box and the strength she wanted.

"I don't need to know all that," Zack said. "Nope. Not gonna do it. Sorry. I have my reputation to protect. She should buy those herself, for Pete's sake."

Shoving the paper back at him, Tanner said, "Fine. Get everything else and then when Deb gets home from school, offer your manhood issues to her as the explanation of why you didn't get what she needed. I'm sure she'll understand." The last was stated with a heavy dose of sarcasm.

Zack's jaw tightened.

"Look," Tanner continued. "Go through a line with an older woman. She'll scan those and never say a word. I guarantee it."

"If I can't get a date after this, we'll know why."

Tanner laughed. "Dog. You have trouble getting dates to begin with."

Both of them knew that wasn't true. With their wavy dark hair, sun-tanned faces and riveting glossy brown eyes, the Marshall guys never had a problem attracting women. Now, getting rid of persistent women was a whole 'nother problem.

And from what Tanner could tell, Dillon was following their dating legacy. Tanner felt sorry not only for the female hearts Dillon was going to crush, but for the parents of the girls.

When it came to Deborah, however, Tanner would just as soon the boys thought her as ugly as a crone. Yeah, that didn't seem to be happening either.

Zack drained his coffee mug. "Maybe if I go early enough, there won't be many customers in the store."

As small as Whispering Springs was, the odds of that happening were lower than Tanner's wish that his sister would grow a large wart on her nose to dissuade the teenage boys.

After a grumbling Zack stomped out the door, Tanner started a load of wash. His mother had hired a housekeeper to come in a couple of times a week to keep the dirt down to a bare minimum, but there was always laundry in between.

"AND OF COURSE THIS IS THE SURGERY SUITE," James Mabee said, holding open the swinging door.

The room had the look of a standard veterinarian operating room. "Nice," Georgie murmured.

"I know Janet gave you the nickel tour last week, but I wanted to make sure you were comfortable with the layout before I leave."

Janet McCaughey was head veterinarian assistant at Whispering Springs Animal Hospital, along with two other assistants and a couple of receptionists.

"And don't forget that Dr. Brian is available to help with on-call. He might be as old as dirt and swear he's retired, but he still loves to come down and see patients."

Georgie nodded. "I met him last week. Super nice guy. And I think it would be awesome to have someone to take night call now and then."

"Trust me, he'll enjoy it more than you will. Now, I've notified all the ranches that we'll be coming by today so you can meet them. I have no qualms about your abilities to handle anything that comes up, but this town has never had a female vet, so I thought this might smooth the way."

"Thanks, I think." She frowned. "Do you really think any of them are going to have a problem with my gender? Good grief. It's the twenty-first century."

Mabee chuckled. "True but remember that many of the ranches and farms are owned by older, well-established families with generations of tradition. Change can be hard for some."

"Well, welcome to the new world," she said with a smile. "Don't worry. I'll make sure the old guys love me."

"I have no doubt," James said.

They loaded up into the clinic's mobile vet van and headed out.

"How many ranches are we going to hit today?"

"I'm hoping for ten at least, maybe fifteen. It's not the number that's the problem, but how spread out they all are. Some of these ranches are comprised of thousands of acres, so driving from one to the next is time-consuming."

"Got it. How often do you have to go to the patient instead of the patient coming to you?"

They discussed his usual schedule, surgery on Wednesdays, half-days on Saturdays and such. The time passed quickly and before she realized it, they were turning into the gravel drive of Flying Eagle Cattle Company.

"This place belongs to the Marshall family. Shoot, I guess they only go back two generations here." He grinned. "One of our newer families."

The drive, while dirt and gravel, was well-maintained. Both sides were lined with fence, and beyond the fence, fat cattle stood under shade trees or belly-deep in the ponds. The grass was wilted, but the cattle that were eating seemed to like it just fine.

As they made the final turn, a large, white, two-story farm house came into view. Well-kept, the house sported fresh paint, a wrap-around porch with over-sized rocking chairs and flower boxes dotting all the windows. An ancient oak spread thick limbs over the drive and house providing protection from the baking sun overhead.

A few hundred yards away, a red barn with a tin roof stood with the doors open and straw strewn on the ground. A man with thick dark hair pushed a wheelbarrow laden with straw-infused manure through the barn doors and stopped. After setting it down, he rose to his full height and Georgie realized he was very tall, much like the firefighter from yesterday.

He waved and headed toward the clinic van, a welcoming smile crossing his face.

Georgie's breath caught. It *was* the rude fireman from yesterday. What was he doing here pretending to be a cowboy?

"James," the man said, his hand outstretched. "Good to see you."

"Morning, Tanner. I told you I'd be bringing Dr. Greyson around." Mabee turned back toward the van. "Georgie. This is Tanner Marshall. Tanner, this is Dr. Greyson."

Georgie stepped from the passenger side, rounded the van's hood and extended her hand.

"I believe we've met."

The smile on Tanner's face faltered. "You."

"Me," Georgie agreed.

Mabee's face contorted into confusion. "You two know each other?"

Georgie lowered her hand and turned to Mabee. "I had a little trouble at the house yesterday. Nothing serious," she hurried to add. "Mr. Marshall here came by and gave me a hand."

Mabee's hunched shoulders relaxed. "Ah. Then. Good thing you've already met, given you're neighbors and all."

Tanner Marshall remained mute with his stunned expression in place.

"Neighbors? That can't be right. The place I'm renting is over on Albright Road. We're on Marshall Road, right?"

"Correct," James said and then pointed toward a

field with an obviously pregnant mare watching them. "As the crow flies, your place is that way. It butts up to the back end of the Flying Eagle."

"It's easy to get turned around," Tanner said, his first words. "In fact, James, all these back roads to the ranches are mostly not labeled. Might be better if the lady stayed with your city practice and you let old Doc Brian take care of whatever needs doing out here. He knows these roads like the veins on the back of his hand."

Georgie's back stiffened. "This *lady* is a doctor of veterinary medicine. Not only can I handle large animal medicine, I enjoy it. If I need Dr. Brian to cover the town clinic while I'm out here in the country, I'll be the one to make that determination."

"Now, don't get your drawers in a twist," Tanner said, his tone a little too condescending. "I just meant that it can be easy to get lost on all the unmarked, dirt roads."

"Not only are my *drawers* not in a twist, you're making a huge assumption that I'm wearing any, and that is something you'll never personally know."

James Mabee's head had twisted back and forth between Tanner and her as though watching the championship match at Wimbledon.

"Don't worry, lady—"

"Dr. Greyson," she interrupted.

"Dr. Greyson," Tanner acknowledged. "Your underthings are not of interest. However, the possibility of you burning down my ranch is."

"Excuse me?" Mabee said, a frown furrowing his brow. "I think I'm missing something here."

Georgie waved her hand as though swatting away a mosquito. "I had a little fire yesterday and Cowboy Fireman overreacted."

"Firefighter, not fireman," Tanner corrected. "A fireman would start the fire. That would be you. A firefighter would control and extinguish the fire. That would be me."

Georgie rolled her eyes. "Whatever."

The three adults were standing there, all probably trying to figure out what to say when a white truck covered in dirt and dried mud clots came flying into the drive. A younger version of Tanner Marshall jumped out of the driver's seat.

"You must be Dr. Greyson. Heard all about you in town just now," he said, walking toward her with his hand extended. "I'm Zack Marshall. I'm the good-looking Marshall."

Georgie laughed and shook his hand. "I'm Georgina Greyson. My friends call me Georgie."

"Since I think we'll be good friends, Georgie it is," he said, a wide smile brightening his face. "Have you had a chance to meet Jolene?"

"Jolene?"

"God, Tanner. You haven't even introduced her to Jolene?" Zack rolled his eyes in a dramatic gesture. "Tanner might be the oldest but obviously our parents did a terrible job trainin' manners into him." Georgie laughed as the gregarious man tucked her hand into the crook of his arm. "Let me do the honors."

They walked over to the corral where a shiny, black beauty watched them. The mare's sides protruded with an obvious late-term pregnancy.

"Jolene," Zack said seriously. "This is Dr. Greyson, your new doctor. Georgie, this is Jolene."

"Oh, she's beautiful," Georgie said. "I love her name. Jolene is one of my favorite songs."

Zack smiled. "My mom's too."

"How far along is she?" She glanced back at Mabee.

"She's got about four weeks left," Mabee said, joining them at the fence.

"I'm a little surprised to have a pregnant mare under my care at this time of the year."

"Unusual, yes but not unprecedented. The stud Tanner wanted to use wasn't available for a spring delivery, we stimulated Jolene into a fall cycle for breeding."

Georgie nodded. "I've studied the concept of doing that, but haven't ever done it myself. How is she doing?"

"So far, a totally uneventful pregnancy," Mabee replied.

"Just the way we like 'em," Georgie said. "I should have brought along some treats today."

A hand shot into view with a ruby red apple resting in the palm. "Jolene has a passion for these."

Georgie looked into Tanner's soulful blue eyes. Her heart flipped over at the care she saw there for his horse.

"She loves apples." Pulling a knife from his front

pocket, he quickly cut the apple into quarters. "But trust me, she'll use you just for the treats."

Georgie laughed. "I'd like to go in and examine her."

Tanner gave a sharp nod and lifted the latch holding the gate closed. "I'll go with you."

His deep voice with its southern drawl almost sent her to her knees. Growing up in the wilds of Maine, she'd never heard anything as sexy as the molasses-thick accent of Tanner Marshall.

She picked a couple of quarters of apple and headed for Jolene. "How old is she?"

"Turned four a couple of months ago."

She nodded. "Good morning, little momma," she cooed. "How about a little apple for a morning snack?"

Holding out the palm of her hand with the apple quarter, she approached the horse slowly. Jolene's big eyes watched her with a nervous edge.

"Don't blame you for being a little leery. I'm a new person, but we're going to be good friends."

She kept her voice calm, and as soothing as possible. Jolene held her ground and let Georgie get next to her. Her nostrils flared as she sniffed at the apple before using her teeth to gently lift it from Georgie's hand. Georgie smiled and ran her hand down the mare's neck.

"Good girl." She continued to talk to Jolene in a quiet voice as she felt along the horse's sides. "Hello, baby." When she spoke, the foal kicked against her hands. "Active one, huh?"

"The little guy has given his mom lots of kicks lately," Tanner said. "I think she's tired of being pregnant."

Georgie chuckled. "From what I hear, most women are by this time. And you're going to be a great momma, right Jolene?" She looked toward Mabee. "You got a stethoscope on you? I'd like to check out our little momma while I'm here."

James pulled one from his pocket. With long strides, Tanner had the scope and was back at her side in seconds.

"Thanks."

He only nodded in reply.

She listened to both Jolene and her baby's heartbeats. Both were strong and regular. The foal was active, kicking against the stethoscope bell and producing a loud THUMP in Georgie's ears. From her initial assessment, Jolene was a strong, healthy mare who should have no problems.

"She's as healthy as a horse," she joked.

Tanner didn't laugh, but she might have seen a twitch at the corner of his mouth.

"The foal's pretty active too," she added.

"Foal's been active for a while," Zack said from the fence. "We might be starting our own line of broncs if that little guy is any indication."

Georgie laughed.

Before she left the corral, she fed the rest of the apple to Jolene, who gobbled the last three pieces with the enthusiasm she had for the first one.

"Have you set up a place for the foaling?"

Tanner nodded while Zack answered, "Yup. Want to see it?"

Georgie looked at Mabee, who shook his head. "We need to get moving, guys. We've got a number of ranches to visit today. I'm sure Dr. Greyson can make it back by before Jolene foals and you can show her the set-up."

Tanner opened the gate to let Georgie back into the yard.

"I'd love to check on Jolene again," Georgie said.

"Anytime, Georgie," Zack said.

"We don't want to keep you any longer," Tanner said. "James, good to see you as always. Have a great time in Australia. Dr. Greyson, it was a pleasure to see you without matches in your hand." He touched the brim of his hat. "If you'll excuse me, I need to finish my chores." He started to leave and then turned back. "Make sure we have a direct phone number for Dr. Brian…just in case, you know?"

His last comment knocked her back like a kick from a horse. She'd thought the visit had gone well. Obviously, she'd been wrong. It was hard to believe that in this day and time a man as intelligent as Tanner Marshall appeared could let the lack of a penis be the deciding factor of a person's qualifications.

She and Mabee visited ten additional ranches. Her reception at all of them was friendly, but she got the distinct impression that her abilities as a large animal vet were suspect for most of the men. The women she met were a little more accepting.

"Looks like I'm going to have to prove myself around here."

Mabee snorted lightly. "I warned you, but I'm not worried. I know you can handle the animals, and their menfolk."

"I think so," she said with a laugh.

The only man that gave her cause to worry was Tanner Marshall. And the list of ways Tanner bugged her would fill a notebook.

Chapter Three

Most of what Georgie saw the first week on her own in the clinic were dogs, cats and the occasional turtle. One of the ranches, Trickle Down, had called in Dr. Brian for a colicky horse. Since she had more than enough to do, it shouldn't have hurt her feelings, but it had stung a little.

"Have you given any thought to what you'll need on Saturday?"

Georgie looked up from the chart she was reading. Janet, her clinic assistant, was leaning against the office door, a pad in one hand and a pen in the other.

"I usually like to make a list so I don't forget anything."

Georgie searched her brain for what Janet was talking about and then frowned. "I am seriously at a loss here. What are we talking about?"

"The county fair booth. Didn't Dr. Mabee mention that to you?"

"Gosh, let me think." She rubbed her forehead. "Man. Seems like way in the back of my brain there's something about a fair but…" She shook her head. "Clue me in. I'm lost."

"The Whispering Springs County Fair starts on Thursday."

"Am I a judge or something?"

Janet laughed. "Yeah. The *or something*. You, a couple of vets from Dallas and a couple of local ranchers are doing the judging for the 4-H animals Saturday morning. Plus, you're scheduled on Saturday from noon until three to man the 4-H booth."

"*This* Saturday?"

"Yup."

"Well crud. You've done this with Mabee before?"

The blonde nodded. "Want me to pull out the same materials we used last year? You can look through them and see if you want me to take anything else."

"Perfect. Thanks. Remind me to buy you a lemonade on Saturday."

Janet laughed and left.

Georgie dropped her forehead on the desk…three or four times. This was the one Saturday a month that Dr. Brian saw patients and she was off all day. She'd been looking forward to the down time or maybe taking a horse ride or even sleeping until nine.

By Friday, all her clients were talking about the fair and the animal judging the next day. One mother had hinted that a first place in the sheep division for her daughter could go a long way in encouraging her to pursue animal husbandry. Georgie opted to not respond, other than to just nod and continue on with her exam of the lady's overweight poodle.

But the verbal hinting was only one subtle reminder that parents had as much stake in these animals as the kids. By the time she left for home on Friday, her car was loaded with three casseroles, a chocolate cake, a blueberry cobbler, a pecan pie, four jars of strawberry preserves, and eight dozen cookies. There was no way she would, or even could, eat all these. She'd be as big as Jolene.

At that thought, she turned her truck toward Flying Eagle Ranch. She could check on Jolene and at the same time maybe unload some of her goodies on the guys. She knew from her staff that Tanner had been left in charge while Mr. and Mrs. Marshall took a long-overdue vacation around the United States.

It'd been ten days since her first visit but the place pretty much looked the same. She crossed her fingers that Zack would be around, not that she was interested in him. She wasn't. He was a cutie, with a personality to match, but mostly, she wanted not to run into Tanner. Cutie with a personality didn't begin to describe the oldest Marshall. He was more like a heart-stopping hottie with a sharp tongue and no personality…or at least no personality that she'd experienced.

When she climbed from her parked truck, a darkhaired teenage girl exited the barn.

"Hi," she called. "Can I help you?"

"I'm Dr. Greyson," Georgie said. "I thought I'd stop by on my way home and check on Jolene."

The girl wiped her hands on her jeans. "Deborah Marshall. Call me Deb."

"Call me Georgie."

"Georgie. I like that."

"How's Jolene?"

"She's doing great. Tanner is walking her around for exercise. Hold on. I'll holler at him."

Before Georgie could say, "That's okay," Deb had her hands around her mouth. "Tanner, come here. Bring Jolene."

"I hate to bother him. Are they far away?"

"Just around back. Tanner's been getting her used to the foaling area he set up for her."

Georgie heard the clop-clop of horse hooves echoing in the barn. In a minute, tall, handsome and moody led Jolene into the front yard.

"Georgie is here to see Jolene," Deb said.

"Georgie?" Tanner's eyebrows arched.

"That's what she said I could call her," Deb retorted in a tone only a teenager could manage.

Tanner turned his gaze to Georgie, making her flinch from his high intensity laser stare.

He tapped the brim of his hat. "Dr. Greyson."

"Good afternoon, Mr. Marshall."

Deb rolled her eyes. "Good Lord. You sound like the people from Downton Abbey."

"Don't you have homework, Deb?" Tanner said without moving his gaze off Georgie.

"Yes," she snapped.

"Why don't you get to it?"

"Fine," she huffed, whirling around, her long ponytail swinging. "I know when I'm not wanted."

"Wait," Georgie said. "Before you go. I've been inundated with casseroles and desserts all week. New doctor in town and all that. Think you guys might take some of it? There's no way I can begin to eat it."

"Sure," Deb said.

"Check my backseat," Georgie said. "Leave the cookies!"

The teen hurried off to the truck.

"We're not a charity, Dr. Greyson. I can feed my family."

Georgie whipped her gaze back to Tanner. "I never thought you couldn't, but with you and your siblings, I just thought you all might enjoy some of the home-cooked meals. Like I said, most of it would go to waste at my place."

"You wanted to see Jolene?"

"Just in the area and I thought I'd check on her. Any problems?"

Tanner shook his head. "No. Don't expect any either."

"Who was the sire?"

"Blue Rocket, from Halo M Ranch stock."

She thought for a minute. "One of the Montgomery ranches?"

Tanner nodded. "Travis. Runs the best horseflesh in the area."

The entire time they'd been talking, Tanner had been running his large hand along Jolene's neck with long strokes. The horse shivered to the touch and shook her head. Georgie knew how the horse felt. She wanted to shiver just watching the gentle caresses.

"As long as I'm here, why don't I take a quick look at the little momma-to-be."

She moved closer to the horse, which put her much closer to one of the hottest, and most infuriating, cowboys she'd ever dealt with. The sleeves of his shirt were rolled up past his elbow, exposing tanned flesh and thick forearms. Every time he moved his arm, beefy muscles made their presence known. What was it about well-developed forearms that made her lose all her professionalism?

When she leaned down to press the bell of the stethoscope to Jolene, she discovered the position gave her a front row seat to study the worn denim of Tanner's crotch. She liked how the material molded over his assets. She'd be willing be wager the backside would cup his ass just right. And—

"Is something wrong?"

Georgie startled. Hells bells. She'd forgotten to listen to the foal's heartbeat. She held up one finger for silence, listened briefly and then stood.

"Nope. Nothing's wrong. Momma and baby are doing great."

The lines at the corner of his overly-sun-exposed face deepened as he glared. "Are you sure? You were listening for a long time."

She stroked Jolene's side. "I'm sure."

Not like she could confess that she'd gotten distracted by his, um, jeans.

"Anything else, Doctor? I need to get back to work."

"Nope. Enjoy all the casseroles."

He gave her a single nod. "Thanks."

SATURDAY MORNING, GEORGIE HIT THE ALARM multiple times, trying to stay in dreamland a little longer. All night her dreams had been filled with a large, hot hand stroking her flesh. Fingers that had been roughened from work fondled her thighs. Thick, sculpted forearms that held her. A deep and uncomfortably familiar male voice whispered dirty, suggestive acts he wanted to do to her body. At one point, an orgasm hit her so hard she woke herself when she cried out.

She rolled to her back and stared up at the ceiling. Good Lord, what a night. Obviously it'd been too long since she'd been with a man. For the past year, she'd been totally focused on her career. Before that, she'd had Chris in her life, but now that she could see the past clearly, she could see that he hadn't been there for her for a long time.

This stop in Whispering Springs was only for four months. Georgie wasn't looking for everlasting love. However, a good friend with benefits situation might help the time pass.

Her treacherous mind immediately flashed a picture of Tanner Marshall. She shook that off and climbed out of bed. Tanner Marshall was not her friend. In fact, she was pretty sure being around her was a thorn in his butt.

She turned on the shower. Oh well. Another day, another dollar. She couldn't worry about what one guy thought of her.

"MOVE IT A LITTLE HIGHER ON THE RIGHT SIDE," Tanner said. Winston Clark, the volunteer firefighter working with him at the county fair information table scooted the edge of the *Whispering Springs Volunteer Fire Department* banner up an inch.

"Like that?"

Tanner nodded. "Yeah. Looks perfect."

Winston tied off the sign and hopped off the ladder to stand back and admire the banner. "I do good work," he said.

Tanner checked his watch. Eleven a.m. "When are the rest of the crew getting here?"

"They're here," Winston said and pointed across the aisle.

Three volunteer firefighters were hanging a banner that read *A Healthy Animal is a Happy Animal.* Tanner groaned when he saw who was directing the work. None other than Dr. Firebug, herself. And damn if she wasn't looking like Dr. Feelgood today. Dressed in a casual shirt and a pair of tight jeans that were tucked into cowboy boots, there was no question why his guys had headed across the aisle. Then she laughed at something Coy Rivers said and threw her head back, her long, curly red hair swinging just above her nice, round ass.

Tanner gritted his teeth. He didn't have time for this kind of distraction.

"Be right back," he said to Winston.

His boots had a loud clump as he stomped across the aisle. "Excuse me, men. If you don't have enough to do at your own booth, I'm sure there are water hydrants around the county that can be checked today."

Checking water hydrants was a punishment job, right up there with washing the entire firetruck by hand…alone.

"No, sir, Tanner. Dr. Greyson was having a little trouble getting her banner straight. Just being neighborly."

"Fine. The banner's hung. Hustle your asses back to your own spot."

The three firefighters gathered up their tools, grabbed some cookies from the tray on the table, said their goodbyes and hustled across to the fire department booth.

Once they were out of earshot, he said, "I don't mind lending my guys if you need help but I would have appreciated being asked first."

Her mouth opened in an O, and then her eyes narrowed. "Look, Mr. Marshall, I didn't ask the guys to come over. They volunteered. What was I supposed to do? Say no to three hunky firemen who want to help me?"

"Firefighters."

"Sorry. Hunky *firefighters*. Of course not. They haven't been over here but about five minutes so get the stick out of your ass."

Tanner leaned against the table separating them. "Do I need to check your area for matches or any type of fire accelerant?"

Her mouth curled into an amused grin. She snapped her fingers. "Matches and gasoline. I did forget to bring something."

He stood and chuckled. With a touch of his finger-tips to his brim, he said, "Good day, Doctor."

She nodded and turned her back to pick up a stack of flyers for the table. He had clearly been dismissed but he stood there admiring the denim covering her bottom before he left. With a silent wolf whistle in appreciation, he went back across to his area.

"Rivers. You're first in the dunking booth, followed by Brown and then Jeffers. Enjoy, boys."

All three guys groaned. The volunteer fire department was always short on funds. Complete fire turnout equipment ran close to ten thousand per man. Some departments required the volunteer to supply his or her own equipment. The Whispering Springs Volunteer Fire Department supplied a complete suit for each fire-fighter but lately, there'd been a lot of sharing among the team. This meant that instead of keeping the equipment they would need in their personal vehicles so they could respond directly to a call, some of the guys had to go to the station first and get what they needed. That slowed response time to a call dramatically. Tanner and the Chief were working together to raise more funding. They'd secured a federal grant that would pay for some, but not all, of what they needed. The fair provided the opportunity to raise additional funds.

Saturday and Sunday, the volunteer fire department was running a dunk tank. Various firefighters were taking turns on the bench. To show that he was in it with his guys, Tanner had even scheduled himself for late in the afternoon. He figured if four or five guys went before him, the novelty would have worn off and he wouldn't get dunked as much.

"Hi guys," a tall blonde said. "I'm Janet, Dr. Greyson's assistant. She wanted y'all to have more cookies as a thank you for helping us get our banner up." She set a Styrofoam plate of cookies on the table and then quickly picked it back up. "She said that Tanner would have to approve it first." She looked at Tanner with an arched eyebrow. "Well?"

His guys grumbled threats of mutiny if he turned down the cookies.

"Sure. Thank you."

She set the plate on the table and the six guys working with him jumped on the cookies as though they hadn't eaten in years.

Janet turned on her heel and headed back to the 4-H area where the delicious doctor was kneeling in front of a small boy while he petted a kitten she was holding. The child giggled and almost swooned into Georgie Greyson's lap.

Georgie. What a horrible name for a woman. No

way could he ever murmur a masculine name like Georgie during sex.

Not that it mattered in this situation. He wasn't going to have sex with Georgina Greyson. Hell, he didn't even like the woman. Granted, she had a rockin' body with curves that begged to be stroked and hair so thick he could almost imagine it sliding down his body, but no.

Not just no, but *hell no*.

He knew all about women who put their jobs before their families. Women like Dr. Georgina Greyson. Women like his last three girlfriends. That he was attracted to her was totally irrelevant. He was looking for someone for the long term, not someone here on a stop between moves.

No. He wanted more than she could offer, so no reason to start something that had an expiration date.

GEORGINA COULD NOT BELIEVE HOW FAST HER STINT in the 4-H booth passed. This morning, at the last minute, she went by the clinic and picked up three kittens and two puppies who needed homes, not that she would let them go today. Anyone who wanted to adopt one of the babies could come to the clinic on Monday and fill out the paperwork. The kittens and puppies had been a magnet for children and their parents.

As the end of her time in the booth neared, she ventured another glance across the straw-covered aisle.

The firefighters had drawn a large crowd of people as they discussed fire safety and smoke alarms. She couldn't help but notice the shocking number of young, attractive women who seemed enthralled with everything the firefighters had to say. Georgie would bet her last dollar that half of the women didn't give a flip about fire safety. They did, however, seem to have an appreciation for the men doing the demonstrations.

What she couldn't figure out was why some of the firefighters left the booth and came back later with wet hair.

"How's it going?"

Georgie grinned and pulled Magda Montgomery into a hug. "Man, I have missed you."

"You too," Magda said.

"Where's your hunky husband?"

Magda obviously loved that description of her husband as she beamed when she said, "Over there." She tilted her head. "He's talking to Tanner and Zack Marshall. How much longer are you going to be here? Reno has something he has to do for an hour. I was hoping you and I could get out and walk the midway while he's busy."

"I'm done," Georgie said. "I'm waiting for Dr. Brian to come take my place. I'd love to do the midway. There's so much to see."

"And so much to eat."

"Know what I want? A funnel cake. I haven't eaten one of those in years."

"Get this. I saw a vendor selling fried butter on my way over here."

Georgie rolled her eyes. "That doesn't even sound good, does it?"

Dr. Brian came strolling up the aisle licking a chocolate and vanilla swirl ice cream cone. "Howdy," he said. "How's the afternoon been?"

"Busy," Georgie said. "I'm ready to hand it over to you. I'll be back in an hour or so to get the kittens and puppies to take home."

"Nah. Don't worry about them. I'll take them back to the clinic when I'm done. Any potential adoptions?"

"All of them, I think."

"Great. Now you two get on out of here and enjoy the fair."

Magda linked her arm through Georgie's. "Let's go."

"Don't you need to tell Reno you're leaving?"

Magda grinned. "Nope. He's gone."

Georgie looked toward the fire department booth and sure enough, Reno was gone, as was Tanner…not that she cared if he was there or not.

As soon as they walked outdoors, Georgie's ears were assaulted with children laughing, people screaming on the roller coaster as it plummeted over the top, parents calling to errant children running down the dirt path, and the barkers trying to lure customers to their games of chance. None of that caught her attention as much as the aroma of hot dogs, funnel cakes frying in oil, fresh popcorn piled into a glass box and the smoke from various barbeque pits around the area.

Her stomach growled. Magda looked at her. "Hungry, much?"

Georgie laughed. "I'm starved. I was running around this morning doing judging and I missed breakfast."

"Well, before we start on all the junk food, how about something with a little nourishment?"

"You always did take good care of me."

They found a trailer selling pulled pork barbeque sandwiches with fresh french fries. Ten minutes later, they were full of pork, potatoes, and Diet Cokes. They wandered down the midway dodging running children and teenage couples so wrapped around each other they could have been one person. Finally, the funnel cake vendor came into view. Unable to resist, not that they tried very hard, they continued their walk while balancing paper plates of hot, fried dough sprinkled with powdered sugar.

"Yum," Georgie muttered. "I love fried dough, sugar, and grease."

Magda laughed. "Yeah, who doesn't?" She took a big bite and then pointed. "There's Reno. He's helping out there today."

"What is he doing?"

"It's a dunking booth. The volunteer fire department is raising money for equipment."

"So those are firemen in the booth?"

"Yep."

Georgie laughed. "That explains all the wet hair I've seen today. Look at that line of women waiting to throw balls. Come on. Let's see who's on the hot seat."

They got there in time to see Zack Marshall drop into the water, a big grin on his face. The women clapped and cheered as he climbed out. Georgie could see why. Zack wore only a tiny, barely there, lime green speedo and a smile.

"How's it going, honey?" Magda said.

Reno gave her a quick kiss. "Great. Zack is quite a hit."

"So I see," Magda said. "Making a lot of money for the department?"

"Racking and stacking like we're printin' it fresh," Reno said.

A loud cheer went up as Zack slipped into the water again.

"You realize they're cheering for his climb out and not his splash in," Georgie said.

Reno grinned. "Personally, I don't think his ass is all that cute, but the ladies seem to like it just fine."

"How much longer does he have on the plank?" Magda asked.

Reno checked the time on his cell phone. "Only a couple of minutes. You might want to hang around. The next one up will be some fun too."

Before either woman could ask who, Tanner Marshall walked out from behind the tank. Dressed in a pair of board shorts, a tank top and flip-flops, he did not look excited to be going in.

"Tell me Tanner Marshall is next up," Georgie said, her fingers crossed.

Reno's eyebrows lifted in surprise. "He's next. Why?"

Georgie didn't answer but watched as Zack climbed out of the box, throwing kisses to the ladies in the crowd. Then he took a deep bow and left. Tanner climbed onto the bench and scowled at the crowd.

Georgie dug in her purse, pulled out a fifty and handed it to Reno. "How many balls will that get me?"

"It's three balls for five dollars or seven balls for ten. So…" He paused, doing the math in his head and said, "That'll buy thirty-five balls."

"That might be enough," she said as she pushed the sleeves up on her blouse. "But if not, there's more money where that came from."

Chapter Four

Tanner's heart rate jumped as Georgina Greyson stepped up to the throwing line. Her thick hair rioted around her face as the wind picked up. She shoved it behind her ears and studied the bullseye target to his left as she bit her lip in serious concentration. Then she took aim and threw the ball.

It hit his cage with a loud bang.

He grinned. She couldn't hit the broad side of a barn.

Picking up her second ball, she aimed and fired. This ball went over the top of his enclosure.

"Give it up, sweetheart," he taunted. "It's obvious my good looks are distracting you."

He could have sworn he heard her growl.

Georgie reared back and let her third, and then fourth, and finally fifth balls sail. Two hit his cage–and he wondered if she was aiming for his head instead of the release lever–and the final one landed short.

Really, he should have kept his mouth shut but it was just too much fun to watch her get red-faced and flustered when he goaded her.

"With your tiny hands and petite size, you'll never get the ball to the target. Just give up while you've got some dignity left."

Reno stacked five more balls in front of her.

She licked her lips. He fixated on her tongue as it flicked out and back in. A spark of lust ignited in his gut. Where did that come from? He wasn't attracted to Georgina-call-me-Georgie Greyson. She wasn't his type at all. He liked his women tall, blonde and experienced. She was petite, red-headed, and, as uptight as she was, he questioned if she'd ever had sex more than once.

Balls six and seven hit his cage, the ground and finally, nothing as the eighth ball sailed over the top.

He laughed. "Your lack of prowess is gathering quite a crowd. I do believe your city roots are showing."

Balls nine and ten hit the cage directly in front of him. Yeah, he was pretty sure those two had hit where she'd aimed them.

His brother came strolling out from where he'd dried off and changed clothes. Zack's grin grew as balls eleven and twelve missed the target.

"You're still dry?" he shouted up at Tanner. "That's no fun at all."

Zack headed to where Georgie stood behind the pile of balls. He held out his palm. "Give me a couple. I'll help you drown his ass."

She shook her head. "Nope. I want to do that myself."

Zack whispered something into her ear.

"No fair," Tanner protested. "No coaching."

"Nothing in the rules about coaching," Zack said.

"What rules?" Reno said.

Georgie repositioned herself behind the line, moving a little more to the right. Zack got behind her, checked her aim and gave her a kiss on the cheek.

"Go get him," he said.

The kiss shot a flame of anger through him. Zack should not be kissing Dr. Greyson. It wasn't right. It wasn't…he never got to finish his thought. Suddenly, the wooden seat beneath him swung down and for a fraction of a second, Tanner was suspended in air. Then he dropped heavily into ice cold water.

The freezing liquid hit him like a wooden bat. His feet hit the bottom and he stood. As tall as he was, his head was easily above the water level.

In the midway, Georgie was dancing and hollering, "I got him! I did it."

Around her, people were cheering her on.

Tanner shook the hair out of his eyes, jerked his board shorts back up to his waist and climbed back onto the seat.

A lucky shot.

Except it wasn't. The next ball hit and down he went again. And again, she jumped around in an excited dance and the crowd cheered.

After the fourth time she dropped him, she'd stopped dancing and was looking a little bored.

"I'm done," she said to Reno.

"You bought more balls than you've thrown."

"Keep 'em and keep the money. I got more than my money's worth."

She looked up at Tanner, and for the first time addressed him. "Mr. Marshall. Thank you for the best time I've had in a long time." Then she had the audacity to give him a saucy wink and blow him a kiss. She linked arms with Magda, who gave Reno a kiss, and then the two women walked off.

The woman might be the most irritating female Tanner had ever met, but that didn't stop him from admiring the swing in her hips as she walked away. Georgina laughed at something Magda said, the sound carrying to him over all the fair noise. It wasn't the first time he'd heard her laugh but he realized that she'd never laughed around him.

For some reason, that gave him pause.

"How much longer have I got up here?" Tanner shouted to Reno.

"You're done," Reno said.

"No way," Zack said. "I want a shot at him."

"Sorry, squirt face," Tanner said. "You missed your chance." He climbed out of the cage before Zack could grab a ball.

"TANNER?"

He looked up at the speaker over his head. "Yeah?"

"Supper will be ready in about forty-five minutes."

"Thanks, Deb. Be up shortly."

The intercom squawked and fell quiet. He loved and hated that damn thing. Way back before every man, woman and child had their own personal cell phone, his mother had insisted his father install it so she could call him to the house. So from that perspective, the old system still came in handy.

However, once when Tanner had been in high school, he'd worked long and hard to get Tanya Jo Allen into the barn loft. Things were just getting hot and heavy when his father knocked loudly on the barn door and entered. Seemed that Zack had turned on the intercom. Tanner and Tanya Jo had been the evening entertainment until his parents got a good listen to the new radio show.

Now that he thought about it, Tanya Jo never went out with him again.

He chuckled and ran a brush along Jolene's bulging side. Probably a good thing his dad had come in that night. Otherwise, Tanya Jo might have had a bulging belly like Jolene.

The crunch of tires on gravel drew his attention. He set the brush on the shelf. "Be right back," he told Jolene.

Georgina Greyson was climbing out of her truck when he walked out.

"Evening, Dr. Greyson. Bring any baseballs with you tonight?"

She laughed. The sound stopped Tanner in his tracks.

"Don't you think it's time you dropped the Dr. Greyson, Tanner? After all, I've seen you in a wet T-shirt."

A niggle of amusement tickled him. He smiled. "I think we can do that. What can I do for you this evening?"

"I was reading over Jolene's file at the office. I didn't see a note about late pregnancy vaccinations for tetanus, Eastern and Western encephalomyelitis and influenza. Seeing as how the clinic records are as tidy as any records I've ever seen, I assumed no notation meant these hadn't been given. Any reason?"

Tanner shook his head. "It's on my to-do list. Just hadn't gotten to them." He frowned. "Why are you so interested in my horse?"

"I have a serious thing for horses. That's all."

He lifted an eyebrow. "Really? I'm thinking my wet T-shirt from this weekend has whipped you into a lust frenzy."

She burst out with a loud hoot of laughter from deep in her gut. Her arms wrapped around her waist, she bent over and continued to laugh.

"Sorry," she said, her words choked. "I mean, yeah. That's why I'm here."

"What's so funny?" Zack asked, walking down from the house.

"Nothing," Tanner replied. "Georgina is here checking on Jolene."

"Tanner!" Deb hollered.

All three adults turned toward the house where Tanner's sister held up a phone.

"Fire," she yelled. "South's Ridge."

"Okay. On the way."

"Chief is looking for Georgie. The fire's near Reeves's farm. Chief said might be some injured animals."

"Tell him I'll bring her," Tanner said.

"I'll follow you in the mobile clinic."

"I'll go with Georgie to make sure she doesn't get lost," Zack said.

His brother's suggestion turned Tanner's stomach sour.

"No," Tanner said. "I'll get my turnouts and ride with her. You follow in my truck."

Zack opened his mouth as though he was going to argue, but after studying Tanner's face and then Georgie's glare, he nodded and headed off.

"You don't have to ride with me," she protested. "I can follow you or you could have let Zack show me the way."

"It's no problem." He was lying. Being in close quarters with the curvy doctor was definitely a problem, but he didn't want his brother to get too attached to the lady vet. First, she was older than Zack, and second, she was a short-timer in the area. If he let Zack get involved, he'd only be hurt when she left town.

So really, he was doing this for Zack's own good.

"Fine then," Georgina said with a shrug.

She appeared to be as thrilled as Tanner to be in a closed space together.

"Deb, you and Dillon stay here. Stay off the phone

and off the radio in case I need to reach you," Tanner ordered.

Deb saluted with a sarcastic grin. He would never survive his little sister's senior year. *Thanks, Dad and Mom.*

He hurried to his black truck to get his gear.

GEORGIE'S HEART RATTLED WITH NERVES. Not because she was going to be alone in the truck with Tanner. She could handle that...she was pretty sure. But she hated the thought of animals being burned in a fire. And it wasn't just the damage from the burn that could be the problem. Smoke inhalation could kill just as quickly.

As she waited for Tanner, she began scanning through her brain for everything she'd ever been taught about treating animal burns. And then she said a silent prayer she wouldn't need any of that information today.

Her driver door snapped opened and Tanner leaned in. "Let me drive."

"Nope."

"It'll be faster."

"You've never seen me drive. Now get in the passenger seat or get in your truck. Your choice."

He slammed her door and stomped around the front of the truck. A smile desperately tried to crawl onto her lips but she fought back the urge and gave him a serious don't-mess-with-me look.

"So? Where?"

He huffed a cuss word under his breath as his truck passed with a pair of red lights flashing on the cab's roof and a loud siren blaring from somewhere on the vehicle. Zack waved and she pulled in behind him. Within minutes, the equipment in the truck was rattling as she hit seventy down the gravel road.

"He's driving too slow," Tanner grumbled. "And turn on your emergency flashers."

"We're doing seventy and my flashers are on."

"I should have driven."

That dadgum smile climbed to her face again, so she bit her lip. The last thing she needed was to poke the angry tiger beside her.

"Zack is driving as fast as is sane on this road."

He leaned back and crossed his arms. "How old are you?"

The question was snapped at her like a wet towel. "What?"

"Easy question. How old are you?"

"Thirty-one."

"Hmm. You look younger."

"Um…thanks?"

"Zack is only twenty-five."

"Um…okay."

"You realize that you're too old for him."

That almost made her slam on the van's brakes out of astonishment. "What are you talking about?"

"You're thirty-one. He's twenty-five. You're too old for him."

She chanced a glance in his direction and

answered his frown at her with one of her own toward him.

"I seriously have no idea what you're talking about. Hold on. Zack's turning."

She slowed to sixty for her turn and wheeled the truck onto a paved road…finally. Zack pulled away from her and she increased her speed accordingly.

"Zack's a great guy," Tanner continued, "but he's not right for you."

"Not right for me? Really? And why is that?"

"I told you. You're too—he's too young for you."

"I'm pretty sure you've lost your mind. Are you seeing a doctor for these delusions?"

"Watch out here," he said. "There's no shoulder and the bank in the road is totally wrong."

She slowed slightly as they went into a curve. As he'd warned, it was a difficult curve to take. When she hit the straightaway, she punched the gas again.

"How much farther?"

"About ten miles."

She nodded and concentrated on her driving. However, the Zack's-too-young-for-you discussion annoyed her and she didn't know why.

"So," she began, "you think Zack is too young for me. Did you have another man to throw in my path to distract me from my evil intentions with your baby brother?"

Did he just growl? She would have sworn he did.

"Wait. Are you throwing yourself at me to save him? Oh gosh, Tanner. I'm just so flattered." She glanced over, batted her eyes at him and then looked back at the road. Luckily, they were on a straight stretch. If they weren't driving almost ninety, she might have taken the time to study the interesting cuts and angles of his high cheeks or maybe the slant of his nose which suggested he'd broken it sometime in the past.

And then again, lots of time could be allocated to staring into his semi-sweet, chocolate morsel eyes. Since chocolate chip cookies were a mainstay of her diet, his eyes held the potential to draw her into a hypnotizing haze.

All the more reason she should not look over again.

"Don't be," he said in a gruff tone, totally blowing the lust out of her eyes. "I'm not volunteering for the job, but if I did, I can guarantee you that I would make the thought of any other man disappear from your brain."

The smile that'd threatened for the past ten minutes pushed onto her lips. A laugh bubbled up and out, popping the mounting tension in the van.

Before she could respond, black smoke and orange flames leapt over the hill in front of them. In response, Zack had slammed the truck to a stop and pulled to the side of the road. Georgie did the same.

"Damn. Hold on. Let me call the chief." Tanner pulled out his phone.

Chapter Five

Zack climbed from the truck and walked back to the van. Georgina rolled down her window.

She tilted her head toward the passenger seat. "He's on the phone with the chief," she said.

Tanner ended his call with, "Yes, sir. If you think that's where we're needed."

"What's the deal?" Zack asked.

"Chief wants you to go on up to Happy Acres farm. There's a team there that needs some help."

Zack nodded. "Okay. Where you guys going?"

"Reeves's Ranch. Got a problem with a horse there."

"Know what kind of problem? I just sort of like to know what I'm getting into."

Tanner shook his head. "Chief said Mrs. Reeves was screaming into the phone so he wasn't sure. Zack, go on. I'll catch up with you later either up on the ridge or at home."

"Stay safe," Zack said.

"You too," Tanner said.

Georgina turned the van around and headed back the way she came. Tanner held on to the door as she took curves at breakneck speed. He didn't know where she'd learned to drive, but he was impressed with her ability to control the van at such high speeds…not that he was going to mention that.

Pointing to a dirt road about a quarter of a mile ahead, he said, "Turn there."

The sudden deceleration rocked his head forward. He held tight as she swung the lumbering vehicle into the Reeve's driveway and flew up the narrow lane, spitting rocks and dirt behind her.

Becky Reeves was middle-aged with graying hair, an extra seventy-five pounds and had the look of the woman hanging by a thread. As they parked the van, her already pale face grew a few shades lighter.

"I probably shouldn't have called," she said wringing her hands. "My husband is going to be upset with me."

"What's the problem, Mrs. Reeves?" Tanner asked.

"I asked the chief to send Doc Brian. Tommy is not going to like this."

Tommy was her husband—rumored to be the most sour and unpleasant man in the county. Reeves was always right, no matter how wrong he was.

"Dr. Brian isn't available, Mrs. Reeves," Georgina said. "I'm Dr. Greyson. How can I help you?"

Tanner noticed the calming tone of Georgina's

voice. She took a couple of steps toward the fretting Becky Reeves and touched her arm.

"The chief said you had a problem. Something you needed a vet for? That's why I'm here."

"Oh, Tommy isn't going to be happy with me. He…" She looked at Georgina and blushed. "It's just he don't believe any woman should be doing a man's job."

Georgina nodded. "I understand. I really do. But I'm here. I can help."

Tanner had to restrain himself from grabbing the foolish woman and shaking some sense into her. Her husband had filled her brain with some total nonsense.

"Mrs. Reeves," he said. "I know you and your family just moved to the area and you don't know me but I bet you've heard of our family ranch, Flying Eagle Cattle Ranch. Right?"

She nodded.

"And you know I'd never let anything happen to my family's cattle or horses, right?"

She nodded again, this time drawing her thumbnail to her mouth to chew on the cuticle.

"Then trust me when I say Dr. Greyson is one of the best animal doctors I've ever seen. She's the only one I trust with my mare, who's going to foal soon. Only her. She's good. Talk to her."

The woman, obviously scared of her husband's ire, licked her lips. "The fire was coming fast. A few sparks got carried in the wind. One of them hit Pablo and startled him."

"Pablo?" Georgina asked.

"My son's horse. Pablo is young. The sparks scared him and he ran." She gulped in a breath. "He's caught in a barbed wire fence."

Georgina nodded. "Okay. We need to get to him so I can check him out."

Mrs. Reeves's gaze shifted around the yard, finally landing on the drive. "Maybe I'd better wait for Tommy to get home."

Georgina took hold the woman's forearms and turned her. "Mrs. Reeves. I need to check on your horse now. Not two hours from now. Not twenty minutes from now. I need to see how much damage he's done and how much blood loss he's had. Do you understand?"

The woman nodded and her face was a study in fear.

"Tell you what, Mrs. Reeves," Tanner said. "You tell Tommy I forced you to let the female doctor examine Pablo, okay? It'll all be my fault."

She swallowed loudly and then nodded. "Yes. Okay. Follow me."

Georgia grabbed a bag of medical supplies and hurried after Mrs. Reeves and Tanner.

"Wait, y'all," Georgina called. "Don't rush up on Pablo. I don't want to startle him."

She caught up with them at the gate. "Who's with him?" Georgina asked. "Anyone?"

"My son. Tommy, Jr."

"Good. Mrs. Reeves, can you stay back while Tanner and I approach? Horses are so sensitive to humans. I want Pablo as calm as possible and he's going to know you're upset about him."

"Okay." Mrs. Reeves opened the gate but didn't walk through with them.

"Can I carry something for you?" Tanner asked. The three bags she had tossed over her shoulders were bulging and appeared heavy on Georgina's shoulders. Plus, his mother would kick his ass if she saw him empty-handed while this petite wisp of a woman carried everything.

"No, no. I'm fine," she insisted. "I'm kind of weight balanced. If you take anything, it'll screw up the weight distribution."

She flashed him a grin. "Don't worry. I won't tell anyone that you let me do all the heavy lifting."

A petite wisp with a mouth on her. Funny. She was exactly the type of woman he wasn't usually attracted to, except there was something about her that drew him.

They made their approach to the gelding slowly. A dark-haired boy stood holding the horse's halter by the cheek strap. His wide-eyed expression shouted fear and helplessness.

"Hi," Georgina said in the calming voice he'd just heard. "I'm Dr. Greyson. Are you Tommy, Jr.?"

He nodded.

"Can I call you Tommy?"

"TJ. Everybody calls me TJ."

"Okay then, TJ. You're doing a great job with Pablo. He seems calm."

"He's a good horse," TJ said. "Don't kill him."

Georgina smiled. "I'm not going to kill him. Mr. Marshall…" she indicated Tanner with a tilt of her head, "and I are going to get him out of that wire. And then I'll have a look at the cuts. Okay?"

The boy's lips were shaking when he muttered, "Okay. Just don't hurt him."

"I'll be as gentle as I can be with him."

She and Tanner stood next to the large gelding. He was easily fourteen or fifteen hands. Georgina quietly lowered her bags to the dirt.

"Okay, Pablo. Let's see what you've gotten yourself into."

"What do you need, Georgina?" Tanner asked.

"Get me wire cutters out of bag number two and a pair of tongs. Oh and leather gloves. Those should be in bag one."

He did as she'd requested.

"Well, TJ," she said after examining the horse. "This isn't too bad. You have done an excellent job keeping Pablo calm and still. If you can keep that up, I should have him out of this mess pretty quickly."

She'd clipped a couple of places and removed the wire when an old, rusted-out truck came flying up the drive, dust kicking up in its wake. A man with dark tanned flesh and black hair climbed out.

"What the hell is going on?" he shouted. "Becky. What the hell is that woman doing? TJ. Come here, boy."

Georgina caught Tanner's gaze and then looked toward the man and back. Message received, Tanner said, "I'll be right back."

TJ shifted his feet. "Don't move too much," Georgina said. "Just keep on talking quietly to Pablo."

"But my dad…"

"I'll explain," Tanner said. "Stay here and do what the doctor says."

After a final glance at the wire and realization that Georgina was doing a great job releasing the trapped horse, he went back to the gate in time to stop Hector Reeves from coming in.

"Mr. Reeves. I'm Tanner Marshall."

Reeves snarled. "I know who you are. Git that woman away from my horse."

"That *woman* is Dr. Greyson. And your horse is wrapped in barbed wire, which Dr. Greyson is removing piece by piece."

"Ain't no woman doctor good enough to take care of horses and cattle. She needs to be caring for puppies and kittens, and such. Becky," he shouted. "Call Doc Brian." He looked at Tanner. "We need Doc Brian, not some chickie playing at being a doctor."

"First, Dr. Brian isn't available to come," Tanner explained. "And second, Dr. Greyson is more than qualified to work with your large animals. In fact, she's very good with them. And most importantly, Dr. Greyson is here and making progress."

Reeves huffed his displeasure and remained silent. For the next few minutes, they watched as Georgina snipped and removed heavy barbed wire from around the horse's left rear leg. Pablo lifted his left leg and stepped free, and TJ wrapped his thin arms around the horse's neck. Georgina said something that they couldn't hear from where they stood but the boy nodded and retook hold of the check strap.

"What's the fool woman doing now?" Reeves asked.

"I suspect cleaning the damaged area."

Georgina waved at them, and Reeves shoved the gate open with a loud crash. Tanner was tall with a long stride but he had to stretch his usual gait to keep up with the man who was charging across the pen.

When Reeves reached the horse, he dropped to his knee to examine the wound.

"Nice job," he said in a quiet voice.

"Thank you, but honestly, it was your son who had the foresight to keep the horse calm and still until help could come. Without TJ, I fear Pablo might have panicked or fought against the restraint. In that case, those barbs could have sawed into the flesh much deeper. As it is, Pablo has some cuts, but nothing that won't heal. Keep them clean and he will be fine."

"Bah," Reeves said. "I knew that damned demon wire needed to be replaced but I just haven't had the time."

"Tell you what," Tanner said. "Why don't I bring a couple of guys over here tomorrow and we'll give you a hand. Between three or four of us, we'll get this restrung in no time."

"Why would you do that?" Reeves asked. "You don't even know me."

Tanner put his hand on Reeves's shoulder. "Because that's what neighbors do."

After Georgina made sure the Reeves family understood what care needed to be given to Pablo, Tanner and she loaded into the clinic van and started down the drive. His cell phone rang before they got to the road.

"Tanner."

"Fire's under control," the chief said. "Everything okay at the Reeves's place?"

"Horse wrapped in barbed wire but Dr. Greyson got him out and everything's fine.

"Great. Go on home. We'll have the rest of the fire knocked down in a few minutes."

"You sure? I can head that way." He glanced at Georgina who'd stopped at the highway waiting to see which way she needed to turn. She nodded her agreement that they could head toward the fire if they were needed.

"I'm sure."

"Okay then. See ya when I see ya." He pushed the phone back into his front pocket. "We're good to go home. Fire's almost out."

She shrugged. "Okay." Turning onto the highway, she glanced at him. "The vaccinations for Jolene. Do you have them or do I need to do that when I get you home?"

"I don't have them, so sure. Go ahead. He paused and then added, "You did a good job back there."

"You mean for a girl?" She shot him a grin. It hit his gut with the intensity of a flaming arrow.

"Yeah." He laughed. "Better than your baseball throwing." He winked, which made her giggle.

"Ain't it the truth."

SOOT-COVERED AND SMELLING LIKE A CHIMNEY, Zack rolled in about thirty minutes after Georgina left the Flying Eagle.

"You stink," his sister said.

"Ah. You're just beggin' for a hug." Zack reached for her.

Deb wiggled free from his grasp and ran screaming out of the kitchen.

Tanner chuckled. "She's right. You do smell somethin' awful."

"You want a hug too?" Zack grinned, his teeth looking whiter than normal with his sooty face.

"Nope. What I want is to eat dinner without inhaling smoke with every bite. Deb and Dillon held it for us."

"I'll grab a shower and be back in two shakes."

Tanner shook his head as Zack left for the shower. What the boy didn't realize was that it was going to take more than one good soaping of his body and hair to get that fire scent removed. Tanner had been on more fire runs than Zack was old.

"Is it safe?"

Tanner glanced up to see his sister's face peeking around the door frame. "He's gone. It's safe."

"Phew," she said. "His scent remains."

He chuckled. "Turn on the attic fan. I'll open some windows and we'll pull fresh air from outside."

They did, and it helped…some. The strong smell of charred wood and grass hung in the sky.

After dinner, the twins headed up to do homework while Zack took off for Leo's Bar. Tanner turned down Zack's invitation to go along. He'd done the bar scene back in his twenties. Lexington had provided numerous avenues for partying but now, drinking and bar hopping felt like he was regressing in life rather than moving forward.

But his days as a single Lexington firefighter had been memorable…at least the ones he could remember.

He lifted a beer to his lips. Yep. Those had been some fun days.

Hmm. Had Deb or Dillon remembered to put Jolene up for the night? Sure, they had some time before her expected delivery, but none of his family really understood how special Jolene was to him.

Jolene's dam had died only a couple of weeks after delivery, requiring a team of volunteers to pick up the mothering duties for the orphan. He'd volunteered, mostly because there had been a cute horsewoman making the request but also because he'd been a little homesick for the Flying Eagle. As it turned out, Jolene had bonded with him over all the other volunteers and he ended up spending a great deal of time with her. The cute recruiter turned out to be married to the sire's owner and he became friends with the couple. When Jolene turned six months old, he bought her, having no idea what he was going to do with her.

The sire's owners let him keep Jolene at their farm

and Tanner worked with her daily. When Tanner's parents asked him to come home, he did, bringing two-year-old Jolene with him. He'd ridden her up to about six months into her pregnancy and while he knew he could continue to ride her, he felt like she deserved a little spoiling, so he'd insisted no one on her back and lots of love and attention until she delivered.

He headed out to her pasture to see if she was still out, which she was. She immediately started toward the fence as soon as she saw Tanner. He would have sworn she was smiling. Of course it was his imagination, but there was a definite twinkle in her eyes.

"Hey, girl. How you feeling?"

Jolene put her head over the rail to get the strokes she felt she was due, or maybe it was the apple in Tanner's pocket.

He scratched behind her ears and gave her long strokes around her neck. "You are looking like you're going to pop."

Jolene nudged him as though either agreeing or pointing out that her current condition was his idea.

"Brought you something." He pulled the apple from his pocket. She took it whole and chomped down. "Ready to head up for the night?" he asked as he opened the gate to the corral. "Come on."

Jolene headed toward the opening. Without encouragement from him, she headed into the barn and down the aisle, waiting outside her stall for him to open the door.

"Sometimes I think you're just too smart."

As though agreeing with him, she entered her stall and turned around.

"So tell me, what do you think of the new lady vet? Kind of cute, isn't she? And smart too. But I've got to tell you, Jolene, the woman's got a smart mouth on her." He chuckled to himself. "She not my type at all, you know? But there's just something about her."

"Yeah? Like what?"

Tanner startled. His head snapped toward the voice. Zack was leaning against the wall in the stall next door.

"Don't let me interrupt you," Zack said. "Your and Jolene's conversation was just getting interesting."

"Jackass."

Zack laughed. "So you think the new doc is interesting, huh? So do I."

"She's too old for you."

"Excuse me?"

"Dr. Greyson. She's too old for you."

Zack's expression took on a look of intense interest. "I don't know." He deliberately rubbed his chin. "She's a looker, for sure. And as you yourself said, she's smart. And heck, I'm pretty mature for my age."

Tanner rolled his eyes.

"And now that I think about it, veterinarians make pretty good money. I've never thought about a sugar momma but now…hmm."

"Mature, my ass," Tanner said.

Zack howled. "She's all yours," he said in between chuckles.

"I never said I wanted her," Tanner protested.

"Besides we don't even like each other. And what are you doing here anyway? Thought you'd headed to Leo's Bar."

"Am. Just had something I needed to do before I left. Invitation to come along is still open."

"Thanks, but no thanks. Been there. Done that."

"Have the T-shirt," Zack completed.

"Exactly. Got some reading to do."

"Reading? Man, when did you get so old?"

Tanner flipped him off, which made Zack grin.

"Don't forget we're moving cattle in the morning."

"Is that your old man way of telling me to not stay out too late?"

"Nope. Just my way of telling you that you'll be in the saddle by five in the morning. How crappy you feel is totally up to you."

After Zack left, Tanner headed back to the house to make a few phone calls and do some research on foaling webcams. The more he read about them, the more he liked the idea of putting one in the foaling area and maybe a couple of other ones around the barn. It would save him a lot of legwork at night, and maybe even some worry during the day, if he could log on and check on Jolene.

And he hated to admit it, but it would probably impress an almost impossible-to-impress lady vet he knew.

What confused him was why he was *trying* to impress Georgina Greyson.

Chapter Six

❧❦❧

G eorgie loved Whispering Springs. The town
was quaint with a unique charm all its own.
She'd been able to shop for just about anything she
needed without making the long drive to Dallas. The
people in the town had been warm and welcoming,
and for the first time in her life, she felt her first itch to
put down roots. Too bad Mabee had been looking for
a temp when he hired her and not a partner.

Texas was a huge state. She was fairly certain she
could find another town just as appealing, whether in
Texas or somewhere else. One of the advantages of
no family was no need to worry about anyone but
herself. One of the disadvantages, however, was just
how alone in the world she always felt.

What she'd discovered in Whispering Springs was
that the people she met and befriended wouldn't let
her feel alone. Tonight was an excellent example.
Friday night and she was meeting some people at

Leo's Bar and Grill for drinks. The group was a mixture of men and women, all single, all out to have a good time. The sad thing was she wasn't much of a partier. The ear-splitting music, harsh lighting, and loud voices usually produced a migraine within an hour. Her favorite fantasy was to go home after a long day to a warm shower, a cold beer, and a hot man. Was that too much to ask for?

A hot man popped into her head and she tried to shove him away. Tanner Marshall. Whenever she saw him, places inside her that she didn't know existed began to tingle. She didn't dare look in a mirror around him out of fear her cheeks would be flushed with lust. She sort of hoped he thought she used too much cheek blush.

The intercom on her desk squawked. "Dr. Greyson. You have a call on line three."

"Thanks."

She punched the line. "This is Dr. Greyson."

"Hey, Doc. It's Tanner Marshall."

Her heart rattled around her chest. She hadn't seen him since she'd given Jolene her shots.

"Everything okay?"

"It's fine," he replied. "But I've got something to show you."

She frowned. "Show me? Are you here?"

He chuckled. "Nope. I'm at home. You near your computer?"

The laptop screen was bouncing balls from corner to corner since she'd let it go to sleep.

"I am."

"Great. Get on the internet and enter this address."

"Hold on." She brought up the internet and then said, "Okay. I'm ready. Remember I'm typing, so go slowly."

"Enter this."

He rattled off an address for Flying Eagle Ranch and then a specific page. Thankfully, he went slowly and when she hit enter, a webcam link opened. Tanner stood in front of the camera, a phone to his ear, Jolene standing behind him.

"I see you," she said, unable to keep the surprise from her voice. "What's this?"

"Well, seeing as you have to come all the way out here to check on Jolene, I thought I'd make it easier. I installed this camera so you can see what's going on with her without having to come over."

"Oh." She swallowed against the lump rapidly growing in her throat.

"Great, huh? You'll have a front row seat to Jolene's foaling."

"It sure is." The enthusiasm in her voice sounded as fake as it was.

"Well, mark this page so you can find it."

"I'm doing it as we speak." Scalding tears welled in her eyes.

"Talk to you later." He waved to her through the camera and then hung up.

Her office door stood open and she hurried around her desk to close it. Once it was locked, she slid to the floor, her knees bent. She rested her forehead on her knees as the tears she'd been fighting won.

This was mortifying. Not the crying, but that she'd been such a pest to Tanner that he'd felt it necessary to buy a webcam to keep her away. She'd thought she'd seen a couple of grins and had even gotten a couple of jokes from him. The idea that she might be getting under his skin a little had crossed her mind. Well, she had gotten something…gotten on his nerves.

She wanted to sit here and die.

"Georgina. Dr. Greyson." Her assistant Janet knocked on the door. "Are you okay?"

"I'm fine. Just taking a little breather."

"We're done for the day. Floors mopped. Phones transferred. All our boarders have been walked and fed. Is there anything else I need to do before I leave?"

"Can't think of a thing." *Except just shoot me for being an idiot.*

"Joe will be in at ten to walk the dogs. I'll see you on Monday."

"Okay. Busy day tomorrow? Does Dr. Brian need me to come in?"

"Nope. Actually quite light for a Saturday. You enjoy the weekend off."

The clinic grew quiet as everyone left. The alarm on her cell went off reminding her that she was to be at Leo's in fifteen minutes for drinks. She didn't want to go but that didn't matter. Shoving to her feet, she pulled her hair out of her eyes. She was going. If she didn't, she'd sit at home all evening reliving her embarrassment over the foaling camera.

As she opened her desk drawer for her purse, she noticed the webcam was still broadcasting. Tanner was gone. Jolene was eating and looking content. She watched for a couple of minutes but Tanner never reentered the picture. She powered off the laptop and stowed it in her case.

She was going to be late to Leo's but that was fine. Her splotchy face required a stop at her ranch for makeup. At the last minute, she opted to change clothes too. Tight jeans, boots and a low V-necked blouse made her look sexy, even if she didn't feel particularly sexy at the moment.

As she'd been told, Leo's was hopping when she arrived at seven. Live music had pulled in people from all over the county looking for a good time.

"Georgie! Over here."

She turned toward the voice and waved at Tina and Delene, two of the townspeople who had adopted her into their circle. To her surprise, Magda let out a loud whistle using her fingers. Georgie laughed, and her world righted itself.

"So glad to see you," she said to Magda, giving her a tight hug. "You too, Reno." She giggled when he made a big show out of dipping her backwards over his arm to kiss her cheek.

"Oops," Reno said. "I forgot my wife's here."

Magda slugged his arm.

"Ouch," he said, rubbing where Magda's knuckles had connected. "Now I remember."

"Will you get us some beers, honey?" Magda said. "Georgie looks parched."

"Sure. Be right back."

Reno headed off toward the bar while Magda dragged Georgie into the knot of people. Tables had been pulled together. Chairs dragged over. There must have been twenty or more people crowded around the area. Georgie's head swam with all the faces and greetings. Some of them she knew, like Tina and Delene, and some she didn't. But they all greeted her like a long lost friend.

"So, you still enjoying the work?" Magda asked after they found seats. "I still can't believe you're Dr. Georgie." She laughed. "It doesn't seem right."

"You and me, both," Georgie replied. "And yes, I love the work. I can't believe how fast the time has flown."

"Tell me. You've been here almost a month and I've hardly gotten to see you. You getting settled in okay?"

"Yep. I'm loving it here. Small, low stress and friendly, even if some of the ranchers can't believe a, and I quote, 'wisp of gal like me can shove her arm up a cow for pregnancy testing,' unquote."

Magda grinned. "Seen that done a few times. Ick."

Georgie chuckled. "You get used to it. Where's your hubby? I'm dying of thirst."

"If I know him, he's run into someone he knows and is chatting."

"You look happy."

Magda's face glowed as she said, "I am disgustingly happy. I'm talking chirping birds and little red hearts happy. I don't think I ever thought something like this was possible."

"I know what you mean. I am so jealous." Georgie bumped her shoulder against Magda's.

"Well, you can't have Reno."

Georgie laughed. "Really? No sharing, huh?"

"Nope. Great. I see him winding his way through the dance floor."

"Good. After the afternoon I had, I could use a cold one for sure."

Magda frowned. "What happened?"

"Long story. I'll tell you later."

"Look who I ran into," Reno said.

Tanner Marshall stepped to Reno's side. "Ladies." He touched the brim of his hat.

Georgie's stomach flopped over and fell to her knees. Her heart clacked noisily in her ears.

"Tanner. What a nice surprise," Magda said. "Is Zack here also?"

"Of course. What's a Friday night for Zack if it doesn't include a good party somewhere?" Tanner's gaze moved to Georgie. "Georgina, Good to see you. I think this is yours." He handed a beer to her.

She took the bottle, careful to not touch his fingers. She was rattled enough. Touching him might send her right off the cliff.

"Thanks." She pulled a long draw off the bottle. "Man. That tastes good."

Tanner dragged up a chair and put it next to her. "Don't think I've seen you here before."

She shrugged. "I don't do this often. It's not really

my scene." She tried to ignore Tanner's sexy, masculine scent. Involuntarily, she leaned closer to take in another whiff. Woodsy. Subtle. Very alluring.

"Mine either," Tanner said, which pulled her out of her olfactory heaven. "Zack sort of nagged on me until I came along. If it was up to me, I'd be home reading."

"Really? Reading what?"

"Probably a cattleman's journal. Maybe a good mystery. What about you?"

The vision of her in a steamy shower with a hot Tanner naked and playing all sorts of dirty games ran through her mind. What started as a trickle of lust bloomed into a gush quickly. Her gut became a furnace, funneling heat down to the junction of her thighs. Her face grew warm under his stare. "Uh, probably watching a movie or catching up on my professional journals."

"You look flushed. Are you hot?"

Yes, but not in the way he's thinking.

"I'm fine. Probably the hops in the beer." *Okay, she was making that up. She had no idea if hops make you flush, but she hoped he'd just let the story lie.*

A look of confusion flashed across his face followed by a smile. She was so busted.

"If you say so," he said. "How'd you like the foaling camera? Pretty slick, huh?"

The gulp of beer she took hit her lungs instead of her gut. Sputtering and coughing, she waved off his question. What could she say? Apologize for being such a nuisance that he felt it necessary? After he slammed on her back a couple of times—not that that helped in the least—she found her voice.

"Great," she replied, followed by another cough.

Magda leaned over. "Y'all play nice. I'm dragging my hunk of a husband onto the dance floor."

Georgie gave Magda a wave as she dragged Reno out of his chair and onto the floor.

Tanner leaned in close. "Well, I have to admit I'm surprised."

His warm breath tickled her neck and set the tiny stereocilia in her ears into motion. A shiver tiptoed down her spine.

"About what?" She fought her body's urge to rest against his chest. She just knew it would be hard like granite. Unlike the cold of that stone, he would be warm and so much fun to touch.

Good Lord. She had to get herself under control. This man didn't even like her. She was Reno's wife's friend, and she was the current vet. He had to be nice to her, right?

"Reno can dance."

She twisted in her seat until the dance floor came into view. The music was slow and romantic. Reno and Magda were wrapped in each other's arms, gently rocking to the song.

Turning back around, she chuckled. "You call that dancing?"

Tanner grinned and she almost sighed.

"Not hardly. You line dance or Texas Two Step?"

She was surprised at the question. "Yep. Is this

where I admit that I took line dancing lessons at the Y when I was growing up?"

"Really? Want to show your stuff?"

The music had changed to an up-tempo tune.

"You know it."

Grabbing her hand, he pulled her up and onto the dance floor. He put his right arm around her shoulder and caught her right hand. She put her left arm around his waist and they were off, gliding around the floor in perfect synchronization with the song's beats. Tanner was smooth, spinning her out a couple of times and back in. Each time she landed against him, she caught the scent of laundry soap and starch in his shirt.

And her thought that leaning against his body would be like being supported by a slab of granite? Oh yeah, but even better. He was hard in all the right places, including one that caught her off-guard but made all her female cells want to preen.

It had been years since she'd been dancing, and even more since she'd danced in a cowboy bar. The smile on her face was so wide, it made her cheeks ache, but she didn't care. She was having fun, and she had to admit, it had been a while since she'd let herself go.

As the song ended, Tanner spun her out and back in, but this time, he drew her up flush with his body instead of alongside. The impact rattled the air from her lungs, or maybe it was just Tanner who took her breath away.

The DJ heard her silent prayer and a slow, country

ballad blared through the speakers. Tanner didn't ask if she wanted to dance again. He just pulled her tight and began to move them smoothly around the floor.

He had to be a little over six feet tall. With her standing a whopping five feet four inches, a lot of the hot, hunky cowboy towered over her. Some guys would stoop to accommodate her height during slow dances. She hated that. She always wanted to tell them to stand up.

Tanner didn't bend to try to fit her height. When he held her, her head rested comfortably on his chest. Right now, she could hear his steady heartbeat pounding loudly in her ear. Her own heart was also crashing in her ears, albeit hers a little faster than his. Was she the only one in lust? Or was he having some interesting thoughts about her?

There was no time for those answers or even finishing the song. The DJ abruptly stopped the music for an announcement.

"If I can have your attention. If you're a member of the Whispering Springs Volunteer Fire Department, you're needed. There's a structure fire on Albright Road. Your chief requests all hands on board for this one."

Georgie pushed away. "My house. The animals."

Tanner grabbed her arm and looked at her. "Your house?"

She jerked her arm free with a glare. "Don't look at me like that. I didn't leave anything burning at my house. There are such things as electrical fires."

He arched an eyebrow. "You don't know that it's

your house, Georgina. There are a number of ranches down that road."

She shook her head as gas was thrown on the fire burning in her gut. "Maybe, but I bet you're thinking it's my place, aren't you?"

A loud whistle shrilled. "Let's go," Zack shouted.

"Coming." Tanner looked at her one more time. "Let's go."

"Go," she said. "Go with Zack. I don't want to hear you or see you right now."

Without waiting for a response from this irritating, self-righteous man, Georgie ran from the bar, along with a good portion of the patrons. *Lord, do not let this be my house.* She'd never live it down.

But even as she raced toward her house, she couldn't remember leaving even one electrical item on. Certainly no candles. The stove was electric but let's be honest…she didn't use it that much unless you count storing the bakeware in there.

The drive, which should have taken only fifteen or twenty minutes, felt like fifteen or twenty hours. She'd pulled in behind one of the trucks from Leo's parking lot that had a set of red flashing lights and a siren letting him clear the traffic out of the way, not that there was much to begin with. Still, it was nice to have flashing lights when she, and all the other vehicles in the caravan, were hitting eighty on these back roads.

As she topped a hill, the orange glow from the fire lit up the night sky. It wasn't just a house fire. From here, it appeared the fire had spread to the grass and trees in adjacent fields.

But it wasn't her house. An indescribable sense of relief poured through her. Her blasts of adrenalin ebbed, but that didn't slow her racing heart much.

The caravan of volunteer firefighters careened to a stop and volunteers poured from the cabs.

She stopped also, not sure if she could be any help at all. As the men swarmed past her truck, she got out. It took a couple of minutes but she saw the chief directing men.

"Chief. Is there anything I can do?" she asked. "Get something? Pull something? Anything?"

"Hold this hose for a minute. Marshall, get over here and help the doc with this hose. I need to pull Johnson to give Avery a hand. Shouldn't take long."

Both Tanner and Zack turned toward where she was standing.

"I've got it," Tanner said.

She had to bite her tongue to keep from saying, "See? I told you it wasn't me."

Tanner positioned himself behind her. "Hold the hose out about arm's length and pull the trigger."

"I know how to use a hose, Mr. Firefighter."

"It's—never mind. Go for it."

Georgie held out the nozzle and pulled the water release. The pressure wasn't exactly what she was expecting. The force pushed her backwards until she stumbled into a hard wall, or rather Tanner Marshall. He caught her hips in the palms of his big hands.

"A little more pressure than a garden hose," he said into her ear.

Damn him. A thrill ran down and then back up her body.

"Let's try again," he said. "I'll steady you and you pull the trigger."

She did.

"Good. Good," he said. "Now move the water stream over to the left and let's hit that hot spot under the pine tree."

"Tanner?"

"Yeah?"

"Why isn't the chief more concerned about this house?"

"It was old and vacant, and honestly a real trouble spot for the sheriff's department. Lots of kids using it for parties and whatever. I'd put a hefty bet that's what happened tonight. Move your water up the tree."

Georgie saw the flame trying to leap from the lower branches up higher in the old pine and she directed the spray toward the spot.

"And," he continued, "knowing the chief, he's letting you spray the hose hoping he'll be able to recruit you as a volunteer."

She turned her head to look over her shoulder. "A, I'm only here until the end of the year. And B, I don't know nothing about fighting fires."

"But you are pretty good at starting them."

She almost let her ire flare until she saw the twitch at the corner of his lips...a nice, full set of lips.

"Hardy har-har."

Grinning, he gave her a wink. "Now watch what you're doing."

After about five minutes, the chief came back with Johnson. "Thanks, Doc. Appreciate you pitching in."

"No problem. Unless there are some animals that need my attention, I'm going to head on home. I've got some hungry critters waiting on me."

"No injuries. Thanks again."

Dismissed, she headed back to her truck. Deep down, she'd thought that Tanner might follow her to her driver's door but when she glanced back over her shoulder, his back was to her as he continued to work the fire. Once ensconced in her vehicle, she sat and watched the firefighters work. Soot covered faces serious with the firefighting task at hand.

Tanner remained deep in the efforts to control the blaze. She also noticed that, in addition to the chief, the other firefighters looked to him for direction. And from her perspective—not that she knew the first thing about fires—he seemed to know where to go and what needed to be done. If he pointed and shouted, one of the other volunteers would go wherever Tanner was pointing, no hesitation, no questions.

How did he know so much about fighting fires?

While she and Magda had gossiped once or twice about the Marshall men, Georgie realized she didn't really know anything about Tanner's past.

A man of mystery. Nothing she liked better than solving a complex problem, and Tanner was nothing, if he wasn't a problem for her.

THE FIRE SPREAD FASTER THAN TANNER HAD expected but then, there had been no rain in a month. Add in the dying leaves and dead grass for fall and it was the perfect combination for a wild fire.

The house was a total loss, meaning it burned to the ground, but it had little, if any, value left. Empty and neglected for years, the dilapidated building had served as a siren for teenage trouble. And he would know. He'd answered the call many times as a teen. Drinking, smoking, late night trysts with willing girls. He'd done them all here. And that had been over eighteen years ago.

Even with every firefighter on hand, it'd taken another couple of hours to knock the fire down and make sure it was out. In the end, they'd lost the structure, and five trees in close proximity. But they had been successful in keeping the fire contained and out of the parched fields.

Ten p.m. had come and gone when Tanner finally sat down. Sooty, dirty, and hot, he should have nothing on his mind but heading home for a shower. But that wasn't what was foremost in his head. His brain continued to fire images of the petite redhead he'd had in his arms earlier. Dr. Georgina Greyson was under his skin and he couldn't figure out why.

Shooting the water hose with her in his arms had been fun, if not more than a little suspicious. The chief had been playing cupid, of that he had little doubt.

Of course he'd known when she had gone to her car. The first time he'd had a chance to glance over his shoulder, she'd been sitting behind the wheel watching the activity through her windshield. The next time he'd looked, she'd been gone, but the fire had been a dragon at that point so he could not stop to think about her leaving.

Now, however, there was an urge inside to see her, talk to her, relive the water hose experience. Although he fought the craving, in the end, he fired up and headed down Albright to her house, telling himself that if her lights were off, he wouldn't stop.

Her lights were on.

Chapter Seven

H e wiped his face the best that he could with an old towel he had in the truck.

This was insane. He was filthy, stinky, and horny, and not necessarily in that order. Those three adjectives did not go well together.

His best bet would be to turn this truck around and get out of her drive before she saw him. Deny everything if she ever mentioned it.

Her front door opened and Georgina stood there. He studied her expression. Did she look confused to see him at her house? Mad? Happy? But her face gave nothing away.

She walked out onto the porch and then out to his truck.

"Are you going to sit here all night?" she asked with a tilted head and arched eyebrows.

"Haven't decided."

She nodded. "I see. Well, I have some cold beer inside and the makings for a sandwich."

He would sell his soul for a cold beer right now.

"I'm pretty nasty right now."

That brought a smile to her lips. And oh God, what lips. Full and soft. And the worst part was the twin dimples in her cheeks that magically appeared with that smile.

"Well," she said. "I do have a shower and running water."

"I hate to mess up your shower with soot."

"I've got a solution for that." She opened his door. "Come with me."

Too far in now to back out, Tanner exited his truck and followed her around to the rear of the house. There, she pointed to an outdoor shower.

"There's hot water. Feel free to use it. I'll grab some towels and soap for you." She turned to leave, hesitated and then speaking over her shoulder said, "I promise not to peek. Besides, it's too dark to see anything anyhow."

When she flounced off into the house, indecision held Tanner hostage. Confusion scrambled his thinking. He'd seen her, shouldn't he be ready to leave?

Even in his indecision and confusion, the answer to his question was no, he wasn't ready to go.

She came back out carrying a stack of towels, a bottle of shampoo, and soap. Just outside the shower's splash zone, a small teak table stood in a halo of light shining from a window. She piled all the supplies on the table.

"I've used this shower a few times myself," she confided. "Sometimes after a long day at the clinic, I can come home smelling like unwashed dog, poop, urine, and blood. Even if I change scrubs during the day, I seem to carry the odors home with me. It's probably all in my head, but a good shower before I go inside tends to keep those smells out here."

Leaning past him, she turned on the water and held her hand under it until she nodded. "There. The water's hot. Go for it, Tanner-the-Firefighter."

No more thinking, he told himself. Just do.

He stripped off his shirt and then toed off his boots. When he reached for his belt buckle, he paused and looked at Georgina. Her eyes, which were a lovely shade of jade-green, were now dark with desire. She studied his chest as though there would be a written exam. Finally, her gaze met his. She swallowed.

"I guess this is my cue to leave."

A slow smile crawled to his lips. "Only if you want to." He unhurriedly unbuckled his belt and pulled it through the loops. As he tossed it on top of his dirty shirt on the back of the chair, her gaze shifted to the belt and then back to his chest...or maybe his waist.

Continuing his casual undressing, he pushed the metal button through the hole and pulled down his zipper.

He put his hands on the waistband of his jeans. "Last chance."

Her eyes lifted to his. "You don't scare me."

"Okay then." He shoved his jeans to the ground, fully expecting her to leave.

With a roll of her eyes, she said, "If you're quick, there's a cold beer in my fridge." She turned and went in through the back door.

The water was warm and flowed down his body like a curtain of silk. It took two shampooings to get the smoke odor from his hair. He actually shampooed, scrubbed his body and then shampooed again before he felt like the stench of smoke and charred wood was gone. In all his years as a cowboy and as a firefighter, he'd never showered in the yard, if under the garden hose when he was ten years old didn't count. Yard showers at his age should probably have felt strange or awkward but he liked the idea of leaving all the dirt from the day outside.

When he finished, he dried with one of the towels and wrapped the dry one around his waist. His dirty clothes were piled in the lawn chair. He hated the idea of putting them back on, so he didn't. Instead, he followed Georgina's path and walked into her house through the rear door.

He found her in the kitchen sitting at a table, a beer in one hand and a magazine laid flat in front of her. She pointed to a blue terry cloth robe that'd been tossed over the back of another chair.

"I found that for you to put on. I know I wouldn't want to redress in dirty clothes after a shower."

"Thanks." The robe was obviously for a man. Much too long for Georgina, it would have dragged the floor in inches. And if she'd worn it, the material would have wrapped around her twice. So whose robe was it? And was it any of his business whose it was anyway? Still, it bugged him that she had a man's robe all ready for him.

He pushed his arms through the sleeves. Meanwhile, she got another beer from the fridge and handed it to him.

"Thanks again," he said. Popping the top, he swallowed half of the liquid in one long gulp.

"Hungry?"

He shook his head. "Not really."

"Super." She leaned in. "Now that all my hostess niceties are out of the way, what are you doing here?" Her eyes flashed with amused curiosity.

Instead of a verbal answer, he caught her head in his hands, his fingers wrapped around the back of her neck, and he kissed her. The first touch of her lips hit him as if he'd kissed a live electrical wire. Energy ricocheted through his gut.

Stunned at his reaction, Tanner pulled back a few inches to study her, and to give himself time to gather himself. Georgina's eyes were closed but opened slowly to look at him. A pair of glazed-over green eyes peered at him.

When he went back for a second taste, she met him halfway. Their lips met in a frantic race to taste each other. When he traced his tongue on her lower lip, her mouth parted and he slipped inside. The hops and yeast from the beer mixed with her natural taste, producing an addicting flavor. He was hooked from the first sample.

She pushed her hands inside the lapels of the robe, then glided her fingertips down his chest. Blood surged from his brain to his groin, filling his cock to an almost painful erection. The last time he'd been this aroused this quickly he'd been in high school, when he could become turned-on by a girl glancing his way.

Then she scraped her nail over his nipple, causing the breath to rush from his lips. Pulling away from her magnetic lips, he said, "What's happening here?"

"You tell me. You started this."

"You didn't object."

A slight smile curved her lips, now red and swollen from his kisses. "You noticed that, did you?"

His gut tugged as his heart took off at a gallop. He stood. "Where's your bedroom?"

"That way." She pointed down a hall.

He pulled her to her feet, and started the way she'd pointed. They made it just to the hall before he pushed her up against the wall and kissed her. He pressed against her, growing impossibly hard at her scent, her touch. He was at a decisive disadvantage as he was basically naked while she was fully clothed. Time to change that situation.

He ran his hand under her shirt and pushed it up her body. His palms skated across her breasts, the lace of her bra scratching gently at his flesh. Jerking his mouth away, he tugged her shirt over her head and tossed it to the floor. Her breasts were heaving with her deep breaths. The artery in her neck jumped visibly.

Yeah, he wasn't in this alone.

IF THIS WAS ONE OF HER EROTIC DREAMS, GEORGIE did not want her alarm, her phone, or anything else to wake her. She lifted to her tiptoes to better reach his lips but instead his hot mouth covered one breast, sucking on her flesh through her bra. A lightning bolt shot through her and she shook with desire. Heat flared between her thighs. She arched her hips, pressing her aching groin again the stone-hard shaft inside his robe.

"Damn" Tanner muttered and then shoved her bra up and over her head, tossing it next to her feet. He unfastened the button on her shorts and then the zipper, before shoving them down her legs. She lifted each foot as he worked her shorts off.

Then, to her mortification, she realized she was wearing a pair of white cotton panties, probably something she'd grabbed at Walmart in a multipack. Why didn't she own something scorchingly sexy from Victoria's Secret? She dropped her head on his chest.

"What's wrong?" He lifted her head until their gazes met. "I'm sorry. I've pushed too hard, haven't I?"

She sighed and shook her head. "It's not you. It's me."

"What?"

"I'm wearing granny panties."

He looked down at her hips and then back to her face. "I can fix this." He shoved his thumbs into her panties' elastic waistband and pulled them to the floor. She stepped from them and he tossed them over his shoulder.

"Now, what were you saying?" he asked with a sexy smile.

"I think I was saying continue on."

Sliding his hands down her ribs to her waist and on to her butt, he lifted her against the wall. "Much better," he whispered and he caught her breast in his mouth again, sucking firmly on her flesh. He pulled her deep into his mouth with a strong draw, then released it until he captured just the nipple between his teeth. He bit down on the rigid tissue.

She sucked in a deep breath. Sexual arousal trickled from her, soaking the front of the robe she'd given him. She arched against him, her head pressing into the wall.

"You're wearing too much," she said, whispering into his ear. She darted her tongue out and, using just the tip, traced the ridges in his ear. The shudder that ran through him started a ripple through her.

"Shit. I don't have a condom." He looked at her. "Sorry."

"I've got you covered," she replied. "Pun intended."

"Wrap your legs around me tight." When she did, he took her full weight and began walking down the hall. "Which room?"

"Last one on the right."

She'd put fresh sheets on the bed just that morning, only because it was Friday, not because she'd had any inkling anything like this would happen. If she had, she would have not been wearing cotton granny panties for sure.

He lowered her to the edge of the bed and then continued down until he was on his knees between her thighs. There, he glided his hands from her knees up the inside of her thighs, pushing them wider as he went.

Georgie's heart was racing. The pounding in her ears was loud enough—almost—to drown out all the voices in her head warning her that this would only end badly.

His head dipped and the broad, flat surface of his tongue licked her. Without conscious thought, she pumped her hips up and forward toward his mouth.

He murmured against her labia, the sound vibrating her swollen tissues. When he licked her again, he slipped a thick finger inside, and she moaned with pleasure. When he added a second finger to the first, her eyes momentarily closed to allow her to immerse herself in the ripples and tingles coasting from head to toe.

But she couldn't keep her eyes shut. She wanted to see this strong, virile man on his knees before her. Wanted to watch as his tongue and lips kissed and licked and caressed the very center of her soul.

He continued to suck on her as his thumb stroked across her clitoris. She groaned and ground against his hand.

Looking up at her, their gazes met. "Let go. Let it happen. Let me see you go over the edge."

As he spoke, his fingers thrust deep inside her. She put her hands on the bed behind her and supported herself on stiff arms as he worked his broad fingers rapidly in and out while returning to sucking on her nub. A quiver that started deep inside pushed its way up and out, making her legs shake with pent-up energy. Then thousands of electrical jolts flooded her system. Waves of pleasure rode over her as her orgasm hit her hard. She cried out with bliss as the sensations peaked again under his masterful hands and a second orgasm slammed through her.

Her arms gave way and she slid onto her back.

"Damnation, man. Where did you learn that?" She sat up far enough to look into his eyes. "Don't answer that. I don't want to know." She flopped back on the bed. "Now take off that robe and get up here. I think I might owe you a favor or two."

"Ohhh. Favors. I think I might like that." He untied the belt and let the robe fall to the floor.

Good God in heaven. It was like watching the unveiling of a sculpted masterpiece. Thick, broad shoulders. An eight-pack that could have been the model for the old-fashioned scrub board, because she knew she wanted to scrub herself all over those ridges.

His narrow hips set atop solid muscular thighs. When he moved toward the bed, muscles popped out in wonderful places.

She sighed.

He sat on the side. "Condom?"

"Oh yeah." She sat up and leaned across the bed away from him, giving him a full moon in the process.

He slapped her bottom. "Just couldn't resist," he said with a laugh. "But I'll make it feel much better." He wrapped his arms around her waist and pulled her back until she was draped across his lap. "I don't know how we got here. I only know I'm thankful we did."

She stroked her hands up his chest until she could snake her arms around his neck. "Me too."

Leaning forward, she kissed him, slipping her tongue inside his mouth. He welcomed her, fondling her tongue with his. Then he closed his lips over her tongue and sucked. Her insides turned to liquid as she melted under his assault.

Down the hall, a phone began to ring.

"Ignore it," he said.

"It's not mine."

He froze and listened. "It's mine."

"Someone looking for you at…" she turned to look at her clock, "one in the morning?"

"Not usually. Now, where were we?" He nibbled down her neck until he reached her shoulder.

Then her phone beside the bed rang.

"Something's going on," she said. Leaning backward, she snatched the receiver from its cradle. "Dr. Greyson."

"Georgie? It's Deb. Deb Marshall, Tanner and Zack's sister."

"Yes, Deb. I know who you are. What's wrong?"

"Something's wrong with Jolene and I don't know where Tanner or Zack are. I've called both of them and neither answered. I'm sorry for waking you up but I don't know what to do."

Georgie pushed off Tanner's lap and stood. "What's Jolene doing?"

"Did Tanner give you the link to Jolene's camera?"

"Yes."

"Can you turn it on?"

"Of course. Hold on."

She put her hand over the receiver. "It's Jolene. Deb wants me to look at the foaling camera you installed. My laptop's in the living room."

"I'll get it," he whispered.

He was back in a flash, the top open and the screen coming to life. Georgie had bookmarked the link, so it was easy to open. On the screen, Jolene lay on her side panting and struggling. All four legs were extended. Her tail flopped around as she pushed.

"She's in labor, Deb," she said into the phone.

"But something's wrong," the teen insisted. "There's only one leg sticking out. Can you come?"

"Of course. It'll take me about fifteen minutes to get to you. Can you get Jolene up and walking?"

"What? Why would I want to get her up, Georgie? Shouldn't she stay down?"

"No, Deb. Get her up if you can. That might help reposition the baby. Trust me. Okay?"

"Okay," Deb said, but her tone said she was freaking out. "Hurry."

"Just stay calm. Let nature take its course. Jolene knows what to do."

While they'd been talking, Georgie had put on fresh panties and a bra. Now she pulled on a pair of jeans and an old T-shirt.

Tanner had left the room as soon as he'd viewed Jolene on the screen. She heard the back door slam and Tanner's heavy footsteps as he came back into her bedroom wearing his dirty clothes.

He took a quick look at the screen and said, "I'll drive."

"I'll follow you. I have some emergency equipment in my truck if we need it. But Tanner," she reached out to grab his arm, "Jolene will be fine."

His jaw tightened. "She better be."

Chapter Eight

The taillights on Tanner's truck flashed bright red as he tapped the brakes to make the turn into Flying Eagle Ranch. Right on his bumper, Georgie made the turn seconds behind him. Both trucks skidded to a stop and Tanner was out of his before Georgie had time to turn off her engine. After grabbing a bag of emergency supplies she had in the back seat, she hurried down the barn aisle until she reached the foaling stall. One glance told her everything.

Jolene lay on her side. Her breaths came in harsh pants and grunts. Sweat coated her flanks. A leg protruded from Jolene's birth canal when there should have been two. It was obvious she'd been in labor for a while and there was no way she could deliver the foal without help.

Dillon and Deb were both in with the laboring mare.

"I got her up, Georgie, but she wanted to lay back down," Deb said.

"Great. You did great, now everybody out."

"But—"

"No buts," Georgie said to Deb. "Out. Now. You too, Tanner."

"Forget it," he growled. "I'll stay out of your way, but I'm not going anywhere."

The teens left the area as Georgie dropped to her knees. She pulled on a long pair of exam gloves and inserted her hand and arm into Jolene's birth canal.

"The foal's got one leg folded up. I'm going to have to push this first leg back and get the second leg unfolded."

As she'd just explained, Georgie maneuvered the foal inside Jolene, pushed the first leg back up until she could unfold the bent leg. Both legs then came through the birth canal. Another contraction hit, and Jolene grunted. The head came through still covered by the thick amniotic membrane. Georgie tore the tissue to expose a chocolate brown face with a wide white stripe. The foal's head passed out of the birth canal normally.

Sitting back on her heels, Georgie let Jolene do what nature told her to do. If the mare needed her, Georgie would help. However, in her experience, it was better to let the mother push the foal out without interference from the veterinary staff unless absolutely necessary.

For the next thirty minutes, they waited as Jolene labored and pushed. Slowly, the rest of the foal's body appeared until it plopped onto the fresh straw. Georgie wiped the new foal's nose and mouth, then dropped back onto her bottom and let the new mother take over. Jolene sniffed, then licked her new baby, cleaning him up.

"Is it a boy or girl?" Deb whispered from the stall door.

Georgie looked up with a smile. "A boy." She glanced over at Tanner, who was sitting in the opposite corner of the stall. A smile more commonly seen on a new father brightened his face.

"He looks pretty good, doesn't he?" Tanner asked.

The colt staggered to his feet, wobbled around a little and then he was back in the straw.

"Yeah. He looks fine," Georgie said. "I suggest we all get out of here and let Jolene and her baby get to know each other."

The two adults joined Deb and Dillon at the stall door.

"He's beautiful," Deb said.

"That he is," Tanner agreed. "Now, what were the two of you doing up at this hour to begin with?"

Dillon rolled his eyes toward Deb. That was as good as pointing the finger of guilt at his sister.

Deb shrugged. "I got up to get a drink of water and thought I'd just check on Jolene."

"Sooo, you weren't just getting home from your date? It's normal for you to get fully dressed when you get out of bed and go to the kitchen for water?"

The flush that climbed up Deb's neck was a neon

sign of guilt. "No," she said, but the denial was so tepid as to be a confession.

Tanner sighed. "We'll talk about it in the morning."

"Shouldn't we stay here?" Dillon asked. "I mean, shouldn't someone stay with Jolene?"

Georgie glanced at the new mother, the umbilical cord still protruding from the birth canal. It could be ten minutes before the placenta passed or it could be four hours.

"No," she said. "Horses actually prefer to be alone to give birth. I doubt Jolene was that thrilled we were all here. I'll keep an eye on her with the foaling camera that Tanner so wisely installed. If I see she needs help, I'll come back."

"But you'll watch from our house, right?" Deb asked. She gnawed on her lower lip. "She should stay here, shouldn't she, Tanner?"

Tanner put his arm around his little sister. "Of course she can watch from the house. I'll make a pot of coffee and keep her company."

"So will I," Deb said.

"No, you'll go to bed," Tanner said.

"But——"

"But nothing. You and Dillon are moving cattle with Zack in the morning. I'd rather you not fall asleep and slide off Nelly."

Deb rolled her eyes. "I haven't fallen off a horse in years."

"Jolene will be fine," Georgie said. "Trust me.

She'd rather you all go away and let her practice being a mother without an audience."

The group trooped toward the house. She'd had some thoughts of spending the night with Tanner but they'd never included coffee, a couple of teenagers, and watching a foaling camera.

As soon as they hit the house, Tanner pointed toward a door that Georgie assumed led out of the kitchen. "Get going. And," he added just before Deb went through the door, "don't think we won't discuss your missing curfew tonight."

Deb tossed her hair over her shoulder and marched through the door, her head held high.

"Your sister carried herself like Marie Antoinette being led to the guillotine, if you ask me," Georgie said.

Tanner sighed. "Coffee?"

"Yeah. Thanks."

"I always thought I'd be a cool dad, you know? The kind of dad that all the kids loved. The dad who really understood what was happening with my son or daughter and all that." He started the coffee brewing and then joined her at the table. "But I swear, Deb pushes all my buttons and I just want to lock her in her room until our parents come home."

Georgie laughed. "Tanner." She put her hand over his. "You're not her father. You're her big brother. She's supposed to drive you nuts. That's how siblings work."

"So you know how it is with brothers and sisters then."

His innocent statement reminded her of how alone she was in the world, how much she would give to have a sibling to argue with. Her gut twisted into a knot. She pulled her hand back. "Nope. Just me."

"An only child. No wonder you're such a spoiled brat. I bet your parents are wanting you to settle close to them. What do they think about your moving around so much?"

She pushed a smile to her lips but it didn't help the hollowness inside. "No folks. No family." She shrugged. "Just me since I was about ten. That's how I met Magda Montgomery. She and I were in the same foster home for a while."

"Oh, Georgina. I'm so sorry."

"Nothing to be sorry over. Everyone has been gone a long time." She shoved to her feet. "Now, how about some coffee?"

Tanner felt like a real ass.

"Georgina." He went to where she stood by the fresh pot of coffee. "I shouldn't have called you a brat or…"

"Or what, Tanner? Asked about my parents? Ask me normal questions people ask each other?" She touched his arm. "It's okay. Really. You didn't know I was the end of my family line. It's no biggie."

He pulled her to him and held her tightly in his arms. "It is a biggie. Here I was razzing you about being all spoiled rotten when you are the furthest from that." He leaned back until he could see her face. There were tears glistening in the corners of her eyes. "I'm such an idiot."

She hugged him and then pushed away. "No, you're not. You're a big, tough cowboy firefighter." Opening the cabinet above the coffee pot, she added, "I'm gonna need some strong coffee, cowboy."

While she poured them each coffee, he retrieved his laptop from the office and pulled up the foaling feed. Jolene was standing, as was the foal, albeit on wobbly legs.

"God, I love to watch foals when they are just getting their legs under them," Georgina said. "He's a beauty, Tanner. What are you going to do with him?"

"I don't know." He looked into her jade-green eyes and felt a tug at his heart, which was probably not a good thing. "Can I tell you a secret?"

Leaning on her elbows toward him, she grinned. "I love secrets. Spill."

"I don't think I want to raise cattle the rest of my life."

Her grin slipped from her face, replaced by wide-eyed surprise. "Seriously?"

He nodded. "Seriously."

"So what do you think you want to do?"

"That's just it." He settled against the back of his chair. "I love firefighting but I love being outdoors too."

"You looked like you knew what you were doing tonight at the fire."

"I do. I was on the Lexington Fire Department for ten years before I moved back here."

"So why did you quit?"

"I didn't quit as much as my folks needed me. I've been here a couple of years but there's just something missing."

"And the volunteer department isn't enough?"

He shrugged. "Yes and no. I can't just keep living and working here. I need my own place, you know?"

"I guess. I just haven't had a place to call home in a long time. I've forgotten what it feels like. It's been rental houses and apartments for years."

Her words burned him and he wanted to flinch from the harsh reality of her upbringing. Even when he didn't live in Whispering Springs, he knew he had home to come back to, if and when he wanted. He knew he had family he could pick up the phone and call. The idea of being totally alone in the world was as foreign to him as Greek.

"Now you're feeling sorry for me," Georgina said.

"No. I'm not."

When she arched an eyebrow in question, he conceded. "Okay, maybe a little. It's just that I've always had family and siblings driving me crazy. I can't imagine life any other way."

She took his hand. "You're lucky. Don't ever forget that."

He brought her hand to his lips and kissed the center of her palm, smelling and tasting the lavender soap his mom kept over the kitchen sink. "Thanks for reminding me of all I have. Even a younger sister that

I somehow am going to have to punish for being late."

"That'll be fun."

"Speaking of which…"

"Yeah?"

His gaze dropped to their joined hands and then back up to her bright eyes. "Earlier tonight…" He swallowed and gathered his courage to continue. "I guess I should apologize."

"For what?" She leaned close and whispered, "Giving me the best orgasm I've ever had?"

She was close enough that her breath brushed across his cheeks. Her whisper kicked over the bucket of lust in his gut, spreading it throughout his system. Sucking in a deep inhale, he said, "I was going to apologize for basically attacking you."

She chuckled and ran a fingertip over his knuckles. "I didn't exactly put up much of a struggle, in case you didn't notice. But to the best of my memory, it turned out to be a one-sided event. I like even numbers, don't you?"

"I do, especially when I'm in the second position."

Tugging gently on her hand, he pulled her out of her chair and into his lap. He had been planning on kissing her but she beat him to it. Wrapping her arms about his neck, she pressed her mouth to his. She kissed him. He kissed her back. When she opened her mouth, he swept in, loving her with his tongue.

His hands inched up from her waist until he covered one full, curvy breast. When he squeezed, she groaned her pleasure into his mouth. Shifting her hips, she settled directly on top of his firm cock, which grew longer and harder with each of her wiggles.

He moved his hand to the hem of her scrub top and slipped under. His fingers stroked soft, warm flesh.

"God, I want you so bad," he said against her lips. "I want to take you right here on this table."

She pulled her mouth away and smiled. "And here I thought you didn't even like me."

He laughed quietly. "I'm good at hiding my feelings."

She squirmed on his lap. "I don't know. I think your feelings are quite evident at the moment."

As he rose to standing, he lifted her into his arms. "I want you in my bed. Tonight. Right now. I—"

The slam of the back door interrupted him. With Georgina still in his arms, Tanner whirled toward the door. Zack stood staring at the scene in front of him.

"Now, I'll admit I've had a few beers tonight. And I'll even admit I almost fell asleep at Leo's before I left. But I'm wondering if I'm asleep and this is the kinkiest dream I've had in a while."

Tanner lowered Georgina's legs until she was standing.

"A little late, isn't it?" Tanner asked, hoping a strong offense would deflect any additional observations.

"I left high school many years ago, Tanner. Don't try to change the subject when the subject is so interesting." Zack grinned. "I knew you had your eye on the good doctor."

"Go to bed, Zack," Tanner said on a long sigh.

"Oh, I'm going but I'm thinking I'm not the only one—or should I say ones—headed that way." He chuckled and started out of the kitchen only to turn back with a frown.

"Are you really here for Tanner, Georgie, or is something wrong?"

Georgina turned the open laptop toward Zack. "Say hello to Jolene's baby boy."

Zack lifted the computer to bring the screen to eye level. Nodding, he smiled. "Jolene's nursing him." He looked at Tanner. "Congrats on your first newborn."

Tanner's anger cooled but only slightly. "Thanks."

After setting the computer back on the table, Zack said, "I'm exhausted. I'm sure I'll sleep like the dead. Won't hear a thing. Carry on." He gave a jaunty salute and added before he left, "Don't do anything I wouldn't do."

———

As the kitchen door swung shut behind Zack, Georgina chuckled. "Nothing he wouldn't do? Doesn't that leave the options wide open?"

Tanner grinned. "Probably. Now…" He pulled her back into his arms. "Where were we?"

"I really should leave. Jolene is doing fine. I'm not needed anymore."

"I strongly disagree with your assessment. Jolene might be fine, but you're certainly needed."

She kissed him and then smiled. "I shouldn't be here when Deb and Dillon get up. They aren't children, Tanner. They would be well aware why I never went home. Remember when you were eighteen?"

His face darkened. "Don't remind me."

She chuckled. "I'm actually surprised that Deb didn't question why we arrived together. You might have an answer ready. I bet the question will come up."

Sighing, he rested his chin on her head. "I'll let you go home tonight if you'll have dinner with me tomorrow night."

"You want to take me on a date?"

"I do. A nice place."

"A fancy dinner? Like no jeans and boots kind of place?"

"I might have a pair of pants not made out of denim somewhere."

"I'd love to. Walk me out? I want to check on Jolene one more time before I go."

Once they were outside, Tanner took her hand. It wasn't soft and thin, like the hands of so many girls' hands he'd held. Hers was a mature woman's hand… solid, with long fingers and short nails. Hers was the hand of a woman who wasn't afraid to get dirt—or blood—on them. There was a distinctive difference between their hand sizes however. His hand could completely surround her petite hand, and the effect made him feel protective, as though he wouldn't let the harms of the world get through him to her.

And yes, he realized that was totally crazy.

Try as he might, Tanner couldn't get a handle on his feelings for this woman. One moment, he wanted to make love to her all night, and the next, he wanted to shield her from the world.

"Jolene looks to have taken to motherhood like a pro," she whispered to him.

He'd been so distracted by his own thoughts that he hadn't realized they'd made it to the barn until Georgina spoke. He glanced into the foaling stall. Jolene was munching on some fresh hay while her new son nursed. At the moment, his heart felt too large for his chest. He swallowed against the lump that'd formed in his throat.

Georgina wrapped her arms around his waist. "For all the bad things I have to deal with, it's moments like this that make it all worth it."

"Thank you for being here for Jolene." Putting two fingers under her chin, he lifted her face until their gazes met. "And for me."

She squeezed his waist. "I need to get some sleep. Rumor has it that I have a hot date tomorrow night."

"Tonight," he said with a grin.

She chuckled. "True."

At her truck, he pushed her up against the door and kissed her. She kissed him back. With tongues and lips and teeth, they kissed and nibbled and fondled. He grew firm and solid under her touches. Pressing her between him and the car, his hard dick was cradled against her softness.

"Stop," she moaned in his ear. "Stop or I won't leave."

"Maybe that's the idea."

He felt her lips on his neck as they curved into a

smile. "You're a bad influence, Tanner Marshall." She pushed him away, but the power behind the gesture was weak and ineffectual. Still, he forced himself to straighten.

"Okay then," he said. "I'll go sleep in a cold bed all by myself."

She laughed and allowed him to open her truck door.

"I'd feel sorry for you but I'm going to do the same."

She got in, closed the door, and rolled down the window. "What time tonight?"

"Six-thirty. Unless you want to be the hottest item on the Whispering Springs gossip vine, I thought we'd go into Dallas for a little privacy."

"Dallas sounds perfect."

He leaned through the window for a final kiss. "Drive safe."

As he watched the taillights of her truck fade down his drive, his heart skipped a few beats. Tanner was watching his future drive away…of that he was sure.

Chapter Nine

✿✿✿

By the time Tanner pulled into her drive, Georgie had changed her clothes no less than five times. Finally, she settled on an A-line skirt, starched white blouse and a long fringe vest that hit a good five inches below her skirt's hem. As she slipped into a pair of dress heels, her knees shook, which was ridiculous. She'd been on dates…lots of them. Why this partic- ular one was making her as jumpy as a freshmen going to prom with a senior was a mystery.

Or was it really?

She liked Tanner Marshall. She didn't want to, but there it was. She did. Once she'd peeled back his tough outer layer, she found a sweet, mature, smart man who made her laugh as much as he made her lust.

And that was a huge problem. She wasn't looking for a man in her life. Not now. Maybe not ever. She'd tried that man-for-life thing with Chris, and look how that turned out. In the last year, she'd pretty much convinced herself that she didn't really need or want a man but then this tall, hunky cowboy had pushed his way in and she couldn't help but wonder if getting involved with him was a good idea or bad one.

This stop in Whispering Springs was temporary. She was gone in less than three months. And she had the uncomfortable feeling that Tanner possessed exactly what it would take to worm under her skin and into her heart. It wouldn't be the first time a man had broken her heart, obviously, but this felt different from Chris. If someone had pointed a gun to her head, she couldn't have said why it was different, she only knew that it was.

And yet, she really, *really* wanted to sleep with him, only there'd be no actual sleeping involved in her plans. She loved how large and solid his hands were. Loved how he stroked her, as though she were the softest velvet. And his kisses. She lacked the appropriate vocabulary to describe them except they made her toes curl in her shoes, and smoke come out her ears. She dearly hoped he never noticed that smoke.

The loud knock at her front door propelled her from her bedroom to the living room.

"Come on in. Door's open."

The door opened. Her middle clenched. There, framed in her doorway with the dying sun at his back, stood a man so drop dead sexy, she had trouble finding her voice. Dressed in dark slacks, a light shirt, and a brown leather jacket, was a Tanner she'd never seen. Usually he wore dirt—and sometimes soot—on his face and clothes. This man looked like he'd walked off the pages of a fashion shoot.

"What's wrong?" he asked, looking down at his outfit. "Is my fly open?"

She stifled the snort that so wanted out. "I can't really say about your fly. I'm not close enough to see it."

He stepped in and closed the door behind him, turning off the glare that'd been at his back. "You look beautiful, Georgina."

Heat flushed her neck. "Thanks. You clean up right nice yourself."

He grinned and the impact almost knocked her back a couple of steps. Oh yeah. She wanted to sleep with him, broken heart be damned.

"My keepers let me out of the asylum now and then."

She laughed. "How's Jolene and baby?"

"Doing great. I'm having trouble keeping Deb away. I grounded her for coming home late last night. She announced she didn't care as it would give her more time with Sir Henry."

"Sir Henry?"

"She thinks that would be the perfect name for the foal. And I don't want to talk anymore. I really want to mess up your lipstick."

In two long strides, he had her in his arms and was kissing her like they'd been apart for months instead of hours. She loved it, kissing him back with an enthusiastic response.

Leaving a line of light nibbles and kisses, he

worked his way up to her ear. "Wouldn't you rather order pizza?"

His breathy question stirred her desire.

"Actually, that sounds great." Plus by eating in, they wouldn't waste as much time.

When he smiled at her, she hoped she hadn't said that last part out loud.

"Tempting but I promised you a nice dinner."

"Dallas is such a far drive. Let's just go to the Lone Star."

He cocked an eyebrow. "I thought you didn't want to be item number one on the gossip mill."

"I don't."

"Then it's Dallas or maybe Tyler."

His arms were around her waist which allowed her to lean back far enough to bring her hands between them.

"But Dallas and Tyler are such long drives." She popped a button on his shirt through its hole.

"Plus, from what I remember…" She pushed another button open. "We were so rudely interrupted last night."

The blood throbbed so hard in her neck, her throat felt as though she couldn't swallow. Tanner wasn't saying anything, but his gaze was on the work of her fingers, his eyes growing heavy with lust.

"And I heard that new pizza place in town is pretty good and that it delivers." Another button slipped through its opening.

"I promised you a nice dinner." The strain and gruffness in his voice made her middle squeeze.

"I know, but pizza and beer can be a nice dinner…with the right person."

He slipped his arms down under her rear and then tossed her over his shoulder in a firefighter's carry.

"Who am I to argue with such sound logic?" He started down the hall toward her bedroom.

Hung over his shoulder, Georgie ran her hands down his solid back until she could grasp his equally solid ass. It was a mighty fine ass, and as a veterinarian, she knew asses.

While she was admiring his delicious butt, Tanner was running a large hand across hers.

"Tight but curvy," he said. "Just like I like them… juicy enough to bite."

She laughed and toed off her shoes and left them in the hall.

"Speaking of yummy butts," she said, giving his a squeeze.

He flopped her onto her bed and fell on top of her. "Sometimes part two can be as good if not better than part one."

Snaking her arms around his neck, she pulled him down for a kiss. She spread her lips in invitation, which he quickly took advantage of by sweeping his tongue inside. He tasted like wintergreen and toothpaste, and that made her heart sigh.

As he left a line of kisses and nibbles down her cheeks, neck and finally along her collar bone, he was also lighting bright flaming torches of desire inside her.

"You have too many clothes on," she said.

"I think that's supposed to be my line."

She laughed and pushed him up. Given his size versus her size, if he didn't want to move, he wouldn't. She might have better luck pushing her truck to town. But he stood when she pushed. She scooted up on the bed and leaned against the headboard.

"What?" he asked, his brow furrowed.

"I want to watch."

Grinning, he slowly lowered his jacket back over his shoulders and down his arms. He caught the sleeve with one hand, whirled it over his head, and let it fly into a chair in the corner.

She clapped. "More. More."

He jerked his shirt from his slacks. Most of the buttons were already undone, so he pulled it over his head and flung it, landing the shirt on his jacket.

"I'm feeling so objectified," he said. The twinkle in his eyes and the twitch of a smile at the corners of his lips assured her that he was in on her little game and didn't mind a bit.

"Oh goody. Go on."

He rolled his eyes as he tried to toe off his boots to no avail.

"Come here," she said, and patted the side of the mattress. "Impossible to toe off boots."

He sat down and she clamored off the bed.

"Give me your foot."

He lifted one boot and she pulled it off along with his sock. They repeated the action for the other boot. When she stood, he pulled her firmly against his thick slab of a chest. Her hands were trapped between them, so she fingered her nails through the hair on his chest. The texture was coarse and rough and felt wonderful to the touch.

"You're sure you want to do this?" he asked.

"I'm sure."

He slipped his fingers under her blouse and pulled it over her head. She lifted her arms so he could remove it.

"So pretty." His gaze left her face and slid down to her white lace bra. He covered both breasts with his hands. Heat burned through the lace onto her flesh. Her breath picked up along with her heart rate. For a couple of minutes, he massaged and fondled and then lowered his mouth to pull a lace-covered breast into his mouth and sucked. The direct connection between her breast and her sex tugged.

Her head dropped back and she groaned.

He unfastened the bra and she let it skitter down her arms until it dropped onto the floor.

"So much better," he murmured, his lips moving softly over her skin. He drew her back into his mouth, his tongue licking the underside.

Her knees wobbled from the sensory overload. He was doing all the work while she just stood there. That would never do. She needed to touch and stroke and taste every square inch of his flesh.

She dislodged his mouth, her breast shiny with his saliva. With quick work, Georgie unzipped her skirt and let it fall to the floor. Unlike last night's granny panty disaster, tonight she wore a lace thong that she'd bought today. It wasn't the most comfortable item of clothing she'd ever put on, but if it could produce the dark, heavy lidded desire in his gaze, she might have to buy stock in the brand.

"Holy shit, babe. If I'd have known what you wore under that skirt, or rather what little you had under there, I'd have thrown you over my shoulder the minute I walked in the door."

Stepping between his wide-spread thighs, she licked her lips and tasted Tanner…her new favorite flavor. "Yeah? I might have liked that." Her voice was thick and deep and sounded nothing like her. Whomever this woman was who'd taken over her body, Georgie ceded control.

Tanner put his hands on the globes of her ass while she slid hers up his unyielding, thick thighs. A large bulge had shoved his zipper into an arch. She allowed her hand to leave his leg and brush across his fly. He sucked in his breath.

"Nice pants," she said in a crumbly voice. "But they really have to go."

She made fast work of his belt buckle, button and then lowered his zipper.

"Careful," he said with a hiss. "Delicate merchandise."

"Doesn't feel delicate." Pushing her hand into the opening, she grasped his firm dick, running her hand from base to tip through his cotton briefs. "Feels pretty solid to me."

When she looked down at her tanned hand on his white briefs, she licked her lips. Under his breath, Tanner uttered a foul cussword, but then lifted his hips and she pulled his slacks and briefs off in one long tug. She followed the motion to the floor as he raised one foot and then the other so she could rid him of what was impeding her progress.

On her knees, she looked up and saw he was watching her, waiting to see what her next move would be. As she'd done previously, she slid her hands up his thighs until she could wrap her fingers around his cock. Her fingers, long for a woman of her petite stature, couldn't begin to surround his girth. There was a good three-inch gap between her fingertips. Her mouth watered with the need to taste him.

She lowered her head and sucked the tip between her lips. Salty and sweet, she slid him further into her mouth. Tanner's fingers combed through her hair, catching strands in his fists, twisting them with each groan.

As she slowly released him, she ran her tongue along the vein on the underside until the tip of her tongue licked the cockhead rim. She sucked and nibbled along the rim before taking him deep into her mouth again.

In the past, she'd given her ex a blow job but it'd been more responsibility than pleasure. Tonight, she was doing this as much for him as for her. The taste of Tanner on her tongue, the scent of him in her nose and the feel of his hot flesh under her fingers made her swollen and wet with a desire she hadn't had in years.

"Enough," he growled and eased himself from her oral ministrations. "I don't want this dinner party over before it's begun." He jerked her to her feet and stripped her soaked thong down her legs. He must have noticed how sodden the skimpy material was because he smiled and said, "Enjoyed that, did you?"

He didn't wait for an answer, instead rolling on the bed and taking her with him. With long licks, quick kisses and sharp nibbles, he worked his way down between her thighs. When he drew in a deep breath, cool air flittered across her tender flesh.

"Do you know how good you smell?" With broad laps of his tongue, he separated her folds and drew her arousal into his mouth. "Taste like the finest wine," he said, retackling the task at hand.

He worked his hands up the inside of her thighs until he could hold her fully spread for his gaze. Her first reaction was to cover herself but she didn't, letting him have all the time he wanted to look and taste. But the reality of his gaze, combined with the caresses from his magic tongue had her moving her hips in frustration.

"Please," she begged. "Please."

He didn't ask what she needed and that was probably a good thing as words had left her brain, along with all rational thoughts.

He pushed a long, thick finger inside while the tip of his tongue played havoc with her rigid nub. Georgie arched, trying to find that cliff to soar from.

A second finger joined the first, thrusting in and out of her in rapid fire. Her hips gyrated in time to his movements. Tension coiled in her gut, pulled tighter as his tongue lapped and licked.

"Tanner," she gasped. "I can't take much more."

"Then let go." He blew cool air against her inflamed flesh. "I want to taste you coming on my tongue. Taste it in my mouth." And with that, he removed his fingers from her and replaced them with his tongue.

Her orgasm hit her with the force of a train. Her back arched as she cried out. Waves of bliss rolled through her. As her climax ebbed, a tear trickled out of the corner of her eye.

"Hey," he said, his voice full of concern. "Are you okay? Did I hurt you?"

"I'm more than okay. And I'll be even better once I feel you inside me."

"My condom is in my pants."

"Check the drawer behind you. Your pants are too far away for me to wait."

In seconds, he was rolling the condom down himself. He spread her thighs wider with his and pushed his cock's tip in. It'd been almost two years since she'd felt a man inside her. As Tanner entered, she bit her lip.

"Feels so good," she said. "More."

With one quick thrust, he seated himself deep. Georgie gasped from the sudden stretching of muscles long denied.

"I need it fast and hard," she pleaded. "Can you do that?"

"Damn. You're killing me. I'll never last long like that."

"Fine. I'll give you another chance later. Fast and hard."

She left no room for argument.

He pulled out and slammed into her, jarring her up on the bed. She reached over her head and grabbed the headboard.

"Again."

He did. In and out with hard, forceful strokes that fueled the fire in her gut.

"You like that? You like the feel of me inside you? Fucking you hard?"

The next thrust was so hard, Georgie was sure she felt it in her lungs.

"Oh, yeah. I like what you do to me."

The muscles in his cheeks hardened as he growled her name as he pounded into her.

Without much warning, another orgasm crashed through her. She cried out his name as her back arched. Within seconds, he followed with his own climax so powerful she could feel the strength of his pulses.

After he'd dealt with the condom, Tanner rejoined her in bed, pulling her snug against him. His breathing was still a little ragged, which was great since hers was too and she didn't want to be alone in this.

"That was…awesome."

"Yeah. It was."

She covered the area of his chest over his heart with her hand.

"What are you doing?"

"Seeing if your heart is racing as fast as mine."

He chuckled and pulled her palm to his mouth for a kiss. "I think I'm having a heart attack."

She grinned. "Maybe I've overcome your first impression of me."

"What do you mean?"

Turning on her hip, she looked into his eyes. "I don't think you liked me much."

Snugging her against him, Tanner said, "Well, I didn't know you enough to like or dislike you. But…" he added in a hurry, "I was in lust with you from that first poke on my chest."

"Hmm. I might have noticed you that night. So, still in lust with me?"

Georgie was stunned at herself. The minute she asked the question, she wanted to suck the words back down her throat.

"Never mind," she blurted out.

He tilted her face for a kiss. "Yeah, I sort of am. I like you, Georgina. You're cute and sexy and smart. But I'm not looking for anything long term."

She licked her swollen lips and gathered up her courage. "Me neither. This is just a stop in the road for me. I'm not looking for anything right now but someone to help the time pass faster. Maybe a dinner now and then. And a sleepover from time to time. I very much enjoyed tonight and I'd loved to do a lot of that while I'm here." She shrugged. "If you're not interested, I can respect that."

His eyebrows hiked. "Not a woman who minces

her words, are you?" He let out a long breath. "I'd like to see you while you're here."

"I'm leaving, Tanner."

"I get that. I'm okay with that. We'll have what we have while we have it. I can't promise more than that right now either."

For a brief second, his cavalier acceptance of her terms stabbed her heart, but she accepted that Tanner was her transition guy…from Chris to whomever she might go to next.

"And no other women while we're together," she added. "Not a jealousy thing. Just a 'don't want to worry about diseases' thing."

"Ditto. No other men."

"Not even Zack," she teased.

He laughed. "Especially not him. This will be different for me at least," he added.

"What do you mean?"

"I've been back for a couple of years. I haven't dated much, not that I haven't had the chance."

"Oh, yes. Women throwing themselves at you. Such a bother."

He chuckled. "I had a couple of long-term girl-friends when I lived in Kentucky. Seemed like I was always trying to figure out what was going on in the relationship. Like it was a game but no one had given me the rulebook, you know? One of them broke it off with me when I forgot our six-month anniversary. Not of our dating, but of our meeting. Who remembers crap like that?"

She snorted. "I know. But since we know this is

finite, there's no reason for us not to just enjoy it. No mind games. All the fun of a relationship without really having one." Pushing her hair out of her eyes, Georgie added, "God knows I need some sex and fun."

"Oh?" He kissed the top of her head. "Why's that?"

She told him about Chris, the broken engagement and his recent marriage.

"Is that why you're here?"

"Yes and no. It was a great opportunity for some large animal husbandry and to catch up with Magda, but Texas did have the added benefit of being thousands of miles away from Chris and Priscilla." She shifted in bed until she could see his face. "What about the gossip mill? Won't we make the fodder?"

"Who cares? A fling with the sexy vet can do nothing but improve my reputation."

"Not that it needs any help with the ladies."

"True."

She laughed and elbowed his side, which made him roll on top of her and start round two of all fun and no games.

Chapter Ten

The next month passed in a blur of long days at the clinic and longer, sexy nights with Tanner. As he'd said, they made the gossip vine the first time they showed up for dinner at the Lone Star, even though they'd made a conscious decision of no public displays of affection. Georgie didn't care one way or the other about the Whispering Springs gossip vine. Within a month after she left, some other couple would be on the spit, spinning the rumors.

The nights were magical, not that she'd ever tell Tanner that. Many times, she wished she were more like a man when it came to sex…no emotional involvement required. As much as she didn't want feelings for him, they came anyway, pushing and shoving their way into her heart.

But they had an agreement. Shoot, she'd lived through being dumped at the wedding altar, sort of, so she'd be able to move on from here.

Georgie was busy filling out applications for other veterinary clinics with large animal practices. Helping Jolene with her delivery had left its mark on her. Of course she still loved the dogs and cats, and even the occasional turtle, but she felt the call for large animal medicine.

In early November, Georgie headed out to the D&R Ranch to check on a sick cow and, at the same visit, have lunch with Magda. The cow would be fine, lunch was delicious, and Magda's questions were relentless.

Magda set a plate of chicken enchiladas in front of Georgie. "This is the first time you've made it out for lunch in six weeks. Surely the clinic isn't keeping you that busy."

"Hmm. It's busy." Georgie forked a sliver of enchilada into her mouth and moaned. "This is delicious."

"Thanks. Now…" Magda propped her chin in her palm and studied Georgie. "You want to tell me what's going on with Tanner?"

The mention of his name jettisoned a heat flash through Georgie. She grabbed her water for a long gulp.

"Umm…"

"That's what I thought." Magda sat back in her chair with a self-satisfied expression. "I told Reno we'd be gaining a new vet."

"Oh, no, Magda. I'm not moving here. This is just temporary. Tanner and I are just having a little fun. That's all. Nothing serious at all."

Magda's brow furrowed. "Really? Cause that

doesn't sound like you at all. You were always the one who wanted a husband and kids and a dog and maybe even a picket fence thrown in."

"It's been a long time since you've known me well." She shrugged. "I've changed." She shifted her gaze back down to her plate. Magda's words felt as if someone were pressing on bruises all over Georgie's body.

"And what about Tanner? You just gonna use him and toss him away?"

Georgie laughed. "I wouldn't worry about Tanner, if I were you. He's a big boy and he has no interest in anything long term either."

"You're playing with fire," Magda said.

"Nope. Playing with a firefighter."

As Georgie drove away from the D&R Ranch, Magda's words kept repeating in her mind. She had been the girl who'd wanted it all…the job, the perfect husband, two-point-five children, the dog who responded to every command and never threw up in the house, and all this wrapped in a pretty white fence. She wasn't sure when that dream died for her, certainly before being left by Chris. She couldn't even say she was all that surprised when Chris dumped her. In a way, she'd been expecting it since they'd become a couple.

She was a happy enough person, she guessed. It was just that she didn't expect the happily-ever-after ending for her.

It was a Friday night in late November. She had not had a great day at the office. The worst—absolute worst—job was putting down an animal and damn if she didn't have to do five today. Two dogs, two cats, and a horse. Realistically, she believed it was the humane thing to do when an animal was suffering. Emotionally, she felt a piece of her heart die each time the owners cried and then thanked her for making it easy for their loved one to go.

When she unlocked her door, the aroma of spices and meat met her.

"Hello? I don't know who's here, but will you marry me?"

Tanner leaned around the kitchen door jamb. "Hey, babe. Come here. I want you to taste something."

After kicking off her shoes, and dropping her keys and purse on the entry table, she followed the delicious scents to her kitchen. A quiet gasp escaped when she saw what he'd done.

The tiny kitchen table held two place settings of dishes, complete with cloth napkins—she had no idea where he'd found those in this house—fresh flowers and two lit candles. A pair of wine glasses stood ready for filling.

It was difficult for her to see everything through the tears that'd appeared.

"Tanner, what the…what's going on? Why?"

After pouring a chilled white wine into one of the glasses and handing it to her, he said, "Heard about your day. Figured you could use a little TLC this evening."

He pulled out a chair. "Sit."

She sat. And then the tears she was fighting won and spilled over the dam.

"This is…is…so…nice," she hiccupped out. "How did you know?"

"Spies." He grinned over his shoulder where he was stirring something in a pot. "I have spies everywhere."

"It was a horrible day." She took a gulp of the wine.

"I know."

She sniffed and then said, "I'll be right back." She finished the wine and then headed to her bedroom. A shower and fresh clothes would make her feel better. It always did.

While the water ran to allow the shower to heat, she brushed her teeth and stripped off the scrubs that still bore the scent of death.

Steam floated over the top of the glass shower door as soon as the water was scalding hot. She adjusted the temperature to just below lobster boil and stepped in. With eyes closed, Georgie braced her forearms on the shower wall under the spray and let the heat soak into her tense muscles.

A cool breeze caressed her ass just before it was replaced by a large, work-hardened hand.

"Need company?" Tanner whispered into her ear and then placed a kiss on her neck.

She arched her neck to give him better access…to what she wasn't sure. He could have access to whatever he wanted as far as she was concerned.

Removing his hand from her butt, Tanner placed

both hands on her shoulders and with strong fingers, began to massage the knots there.

"Hmm," she moaned. "Feels so good."

His mouth found her nape and nuzzled there, kissing and licking her skin as he continued to knead her shoulders and then down her back. His thumbs pressed along her spine as he walked his powerful fingers down to her hips.

The entire time, all she could do was moan and whimper with pleasure at his touch. Sometimes coming home to an empty house after a horrible day added to her stress but having Tanner here, even temporarily, filled some of the empty places she had in her soul.

He caressed her bottom, molding the flesh with his palms. Reflexively, she arched her back, pressing into his hands.

"Spread your legs," he ordered in a gruff voice.

He didn't have to tell her twice. She widened her stance until her feet touched opposite sides of her rather generous shower. He continued to rub down her thighs, her calves, her ankles and then started back up her legs.

She found herself in the oddest of conditions. His gentle strokes were relaxing her taut muscles, while at the time everything inside her was racing and throbbing and aching for more. A total quagmire of feelings.

The heat from his mouth flashed over her ass, followed by a caress from his lips. She sighed and tried to open her thighs wider but it was impossible. She was as spread as she could be in this space.

He turned the water off. "Turn around."

She did and the vision almost made her collapse into a heap. Tanner was kneeling at her feet, a supplicant at the feet of a queen, or that's how he made her feel.

"I turned the water off because it was washing away your scent and I love the way you smell. And your taste. I love the way you taste and the water would spoil that for me." He nuzzled her coarse pubic hair. "I love your red hair. It's like fire." He looked at her. "And you do light a fire in me."

With that comment, he grabbed her thighs and put his head between them, using his tongue to lick her arousal fluid and his mouth to suck on her swollen flesh. He used his thumbs to spread her open for him, to bare her to whatever he wanted to do. In all the time she'd been with Chris, she'd never allowed herself to be so exposed, but with Tanner, she felt protected and safe.

He traced his tongue around her rigid nub, stopping to draw it into his mouth. She arched and groaned. Her hips gyrated on his mouth, wanting more, needing a release that only he could give her.

When he pushed two fingers into her, her hips moved quicker, demanding he thrust them to her tempo. He let her set the pace, sliding them in and out while his mouth worked her stiff button.

It didn't take long before she felt the rising tension inside.

"More," she cried. "More. I'm almost there."

And then she was at the threshold, tense and shaking before she went over, crying out his name.

He kissed the inside of her thigh. "Finish your shower. I'll go get dinner together."

She grabbed his arm and looked down at his impressive erection. "What about you?"

He smiled. "You had your dessert before dinner. That's my dessert."

He kissed her deeply and then turned on the water.

"Don't worry," he said. "I won't forget where we were."

Later that night, she showed him that she hadn't forgotten either.

"TANNER, PASS ME THE ROLLS," JANET MARSHALL said.

Tanner lifted the basket of hot bread and handed it over to his mother. His parents had arrived home three days before Thanksgiving. He'd been more than happy to turn back over the reins of home and ranch management to them. He didn't have to manage a teenage girl and it had freed him up to spend a couple of guilt-free evenings with Georgina. A total win-win in his book.

"You should have invited your lady friend to join us today," his mother continued. "I hate the thought that she might be alone on Thanksgiving."

The bite of turkey Tanner tried to swallow went down sideways making him choke and cough. "Lady friend?"

The last thing he needed, or wanted, was his mother digging around in his personal life. She'd been hinting about grandchildren since he'd turned thirty.

His mother smiled as she lifted her wine glass to her mouth for a sip. "Deb tells us you've been seeing the new vet in town."

Tanner rolled a glare over to his sister who gave him a beatific expression of total innocence.

Oh yeah? Well, two can play this game.

"While she was filling you in on my life, did Deb happen to mention the number of times she missed curfew? Because I have to tell you, that's a much more interesting story."

Under the table, his shin took a direct kick from Deb's pointed-toe cowboy boot.

"Ouch," he said, leaning over to rub at his throbbing leg.

"No, she might have failed to mention that," Richard Marshall said. His father glanced over at Deb. "We can talk about that later tonight, little missy."

"Tell us more about the vet you're seeing," his mother said.

"Nothing to tell. Georgina's a nice gal in town for a couple of months. She's leaving next month. End of story."

"Hmm. So," his mother continued, sliding her

gaze to another of her offspring. "What's going on with you, Zack?"

His brother grinned. "Not a thing. Working hard. Covering for Tanner while he dates the doctor."

Suddenly, the food in his stomach didn't seem to be setting right. A stomach cramp followed by a wave of irritation at his siblings had Tanner done with this meal.

He shoved back his chair and stood. "I need to see to the horses. Delicious meal, Mom. Glad to have you home." He picked up his plate still loaded with food, kissed his mother's cheek and headed for the kitchen.

"What about dessert?" his mother called after him.

"I'm stuffed. Maybe later."

After grabbing a couple of apples for Jolene, he headed down to find her and her baby. Somehow, Sir Henry had stuck as a name and now it didn't seem right to call the little guy by anything else.

He rested one boot-covered foot on the lower rail of the fence and let his gaze roam over the acreage before him. When he finally saw them, they were pretty far down in the pasture. Tanner shoved two fingers between his lips and let out a long, loud whistle. Jolene's head snapped up from the grass where she was grazing and she started toward him, Sir Henry trotting along beside her.

A heavy footfall behind him alerted him to his dad's presence before the man said a word.

"She looks great," Richard said. "And her colt is a real looker. I wasn't sure about resetting her estrus and letting her foal in the fall, but looks like you were right about that. "

"Thanks."

His father assumed an identical position, foot propped on the lower fence rail, and crossed his arms over the top rail. "Your mom meant no harm with all her questions. She's just interested in what she missed while we've been gone. I don't think our trip was exactly what she'd thought it would be." He chuckled. "You guys didn't call enough, asking for help."

Tanner looked at him. "Are you kidding? I wanted to call her every day and ask her something but we didn't want to bother y'all. I know she'd been wanting to do that trip for years." He removed his hat and ran his fingers through his hair. "I do not understand women."

His dad laughed. "And you never will, son. Hell, I've been married to your mother for thirty-six years and I still haven't figured her out. But that's what makes life interesting, huh? Trying to figure out mysteries."

"Good point."

"But it's not your mom, is it? There's something else going on with you. Want to talk about it?"

Tanner considered his next words carefully as he watched Jolene prance up to the fence. He cut an apple into wedges and fed a couple to her. He let out a long breath.

"I don't think my future is here."

Richard nodded. "I see. Here, as in Whispering Springs or here, as in Flying Eagle Cattle Company?"

"The cattle ranch." He shot a quick glance toward his dad and then back at his mare as he fed her another apple chunk. "Being back in Texas has been…eye-opening, to say the least. I enjoyed my time in Kentucky, but I'm a Texas man at heart, I guess."

"I see. Well, if not cattle, then what? Back to fire-fighting?"

"I definitely want to keep that going. Chief Townsend has been talking to me about taking over for him. He's wanting to cut back."

"And is that something you're interested in?"

"Yeah, definitely. The county will pay for me to go to the National Fire Academy for some additional training." Tanner looked at his dad. "I'd have to leave next week. I'd be gone until a couple of days before Christmas. What do you think about that?"

"I think it sounds like an opportunity that you'd be a fool to give up."

"But the ranch…"

"Your mother and I aren't going anywhere until after Christmas. Maybe even into the New Year. So there's no reason you can't go, unless there is." Richard gave him a questioning look. "Is there anything, or maybe anyone, keeping you here?"

"Did Mom send you out here to pump me for information?"

His father laughed and then leaned closer. "Nope, but if I go back with insider information, I'll get a bigger piece of pecan pie."

Tanner shook his head with a chuckle. "There's

nothing really to tell. Georgina's great but she's out of here as soon as Mabee gets back."

His heart twisted as though wringing out all its blood at the thought that Georgina would soon be a memory. No more seeing her head tossed back and hearing her peals of laughter. No more watching her care for a sick animal with her tender touch and gentle voice. No more long nights of kisses and touches and caresses that drove them both wild.

"No," he said to his dad. "There's nothing keeping me tied here for the next three weeks."

He was quiet for a minute thinking about this incredible woman he'd met. How she made him laugh. How she made him feel so strong and protective. How she evoked emotions in him that he'd never really felt. But he'd gone into the relationship knowing it was temporary. That's how Georgina wanted it.

"How long you been in love with her? And more importantly, does she know?"

Tanner shrugged but didn't answer the question. "Pecan pie, you say? Sounds like just what I need."

His dad's questions rang in his head long after their conversation was done. Was he in love with her? He wasn't sure. He'd said those three words to women before who'd never had the impact on him that Georgina did.

What he did know was that just hearing her voice made his day brighter. Seeing her, holding her, could repair even his worst mood. Hell, the mere thought of her could grind the spurs off a trying day. He might have sent his wearisome sister to a nunnery within the past couple of months if it hadn't been for Georgina. That thought made him smile.

The other thing he knew? Tanner needed to see her every day because when he didn't, it felt like the sun forgot to rise.

Chapter Eleven

"Thanks for helping with the dishes. You didn't have to," Magda Montgomery said.

"The least I could do," Georgie said. "I appreciate your having me out for dinner."

"You should have come for Thanksgiving lunch with all the Montgomerys. They would have been happy to have had you join us."

Georgie produced a dramatic shiver. "Thanks but no thanks. How do you handle all that testosterone in one room?"

Magda laughed. "You get used to it." She dried her hands on a dish towel and then hung it over the sink edge to dry. "Besides, I live with Reno, Mister Testosterone himself."

"Just as well I didn't. I ended up having a couple of emergencies and being all the way out at the Bar M would have made it tough to take calls today."

Magda leaned against the edge of the counter and crossed one ankle over the other. "Not that I'm prying, but why weren't you with Tanner today?"

"Not that you're prying or anything," she said and then quirked the corner of her mouth.

Magda shrugged. "If your best friend can't pry, who can?"

"Give me some coffee. Maybe I could use a shoulder to lean on."

They retook seats at the table, mugs of fresh coffee cradled in their fingers.

"Okay, so you've fallen for Tanner. Now what?"

"What? Who told you that? Did Tanner say something to Reno?"

Magda snorted. "Yeah. Like guys talk about feelings. Of course Tanner hasn't said anything. But honey, I've seen you with Tanner. You get this look on your face."

"What kind of look?"

"A dreamy, dopey, starry-eyed stare when you look at him."

Georgie pounded her forehead on the table. "Oh, God." She rolled her head to the side so she could look up at her friend. "Really?"

Magda nodded.

"Think anyone else might have noticed?"

"No. Of course not," Magda assured her. "They'd only have seen it if they looked at you."

"Argh." Georgie sat upright. "Think Tanner noticed?"

"He's a guy, so probably not."

"It wasn't supposed to be like this. It was supposed to be fun, carefree, scratch-my-itch sort of thing. And at first it was. But then one day, it wasn't."

"So? What are you going to do about it?"

"Not a damn thing. We agreed that nothing would come out of this. We'd enjoy what we had while we had it and then when I left, it'd be over."

"Well, that's the stupidest thing I've ever heard."

Georgie rolled her eyes. "Spoken by the woman who ran from love."

Magda nodded. "True. Stupid move, but still…"

With a long sigh, she said, "Maybe the plan wasn't the brightest idea, but for once it felt good to have someone stable in my life. We promised no games, no bullshit. I can't change the rules unilaterally." The smile she forced to her lips felt awkward and she'd bet it looked it too. "I'll be fine. Hearts heal, right? I'm looking…forward…to…moving." The last couple of words came out with a cry.

"Oh, honey." Magda put her arm around Georgie. "Maybe Tanner feels the same way. You ever think of that?"

"He doesn't." Georgie sniffed. "Besides, I don't have a job here. I would never start a practice in competition with Whispering Springs Animal Clinic. That would be so wrong. Mabee only brought me here temporarily."

"Is there enough work for two fulltime vets?"

"Yes, but I heard a rumor that some vet from

Dallas was looking at vacant storefronts in town with a plan to set up a satellite clinic here and see patients a few days a week. That could really cut into our patient load. But really, none of that matters. There is no way I could stay here and run into Tanner with some new girlfriend."

"First, Whispering Springs is a gossip factory so maybe some vet looked at property or maybe not. You don't know that for a fact. And second, how do you know Tanner isn't feeling the same way?"

"He's just not and talking about it isn't going to change anything." Georgie stood. "I need to get going. Got a long drive home."

Linking arms, they walked outside to Georgie's truck where Magda gave her a hug. "I love you, girl-friend. Don't you forget that. No matter where you are, I'm only a phone call away. And one more thing. Tanner's been here for two years and in all that time, he's never dated anyone more than twice, much less two months. Just think on that."

"I will. Thanks. Love you too."

As Georgie drove home, she thought about her agreement with Tanner. No games. No bullshit. Did that mean she owed him the truth? Did "no games" mean she shouldn't have fallen for him, or did it mean that she should tell him that she had?

Of course, there stood the very distinct possibility that he would break it off immediately if she told him how she felt.

Was it better to enjoy what they had while it lasted and leave town with her reputation intact, or better to risk it all and possibly lose what time they had left, and leave town with a broken heart?

Well, shoot. No matter how she answered either of those questions, she'd be leaving town with a broken heart. The only question then was…did she squander what time she had left with Tanner or should she suck it up, shut it up, and enjoy him in her bed for the next couple of weeks?

Tanner surprised her by being at her house when she got home. She'd given him a key a few weeks back and he used it often to surprise her with dinner. But not tonight since she suspected he was as stuffed as she from Thanksgiving meals.

"Hey,'" she said upon finding him sitting on her couch. "What's up?"

"Can't I just come by and see my gal without something being up?"

She dropped her purse and keys on the entry table and hung up her jacket. Hearing him call her *my gal* sent her gut into a little spin.

She sat beside him and wrapped her arms around his neck. "You can. And this gal is glad to see you." She kissed him, his soft lips tasting like the finest wine.

"I missed you today," he said, as he pulled her into a tight embrace.

"Me too. How is having your folks home?"

"I may never let them leave again."

She chuckled and snuggled in close. "You here for the night?" She held up crossed fingers.

"Let's go away for a couple of days."

She struggled upright and looked at him. "Go

away? Where? When?" She shook her head. "I don't know, Tanner. The clinic…"

"Maybe I shouldn't have, but I called Dr. Brian about this weekend. He said he'd be glad to cover Saturday and Sunday. We can head out when you get done on Friday." He kissed her, his nibbles on her lips driving her crazy. "Don't say no. It'll be just the two of us. No animals to feed. No younger siblings to wrangle."

"But what about the animals here at this ranch? Granted, I'm only babysitting them, but I can't go off and leave them all nilly-willy."

"If I can get Zack to take care of them, then would you go?"

"Maybe."

"Fine. Zack has already agreed to come stay here. I think he liked the idea of the privacy. With the parents home again, he and I are free as birds."

She poked his ribs. "You already had all my objections covered, didn't you?"

He tickled her back and when she squirmed, took advantage to get her on her back with him on top. "Yep. I know how that brain of yours thinks."

"Well, that's scary."

"Tell me," he said with a laugh but then his face grew serious. "I want this time together. Just us. Will you go?"

"How can I say no?"

All day Friday Georgie thought about the trip, wondering about the suddenness, not that she was complaining. Two whole days of just Tanner—preferably a naked Tanner—sounded perfect.

She saw the last pet of the day and then went into her office to freshen up before Tanner arrived. All day she'd thought about what Magda had said yesterday… Tanner had never dated anyone as long as he'd been with Georgie.

Oh. My. God. He was taking her away for the weekend to propose. That had to be it. Her heart shot off like a rocket. How should she react? Surprised, of course. Maybe a little stunned.

She pulled a mirror from her purse and practiced a couple of expressions.

Letting her mouth gape in surprise, she opened her eyes wide in shock. No, that one made her look like a guppy.

She kept her mouth closed but smiled while opening her eyes wide. That one wasn't too bad. She practiced it a couple of more times.

Hmm. Should she say yes immediately? Or pretend she had to think about it?

Her gut clenched and she wrapped her arms around her waist. Oh. My. God. Tanner was going to ask her to marry him.

About to burst with excitement, Georgie grabbed the phone to call Magda, but before she could dial, Tanner knocked on her door.

"Oh, sorry," he said after he stuck his head in the door. "Didn't know you were on the phone. I'll wait outside."

She quickly replaced the receiver. Damn. She almost ruined her own surprise.

"I'm done. Let me grab my purse, and get my bag from my truck and we'll be off."

He stepped into her office filling the space with all his yummy testosterone and closed the door.

Oh dear. Was he going to ask her right now? "What's wrong?"

He smiled and pulled her into a warm embrace. "Not a damn thing. I can't wait to get you all to myself." He kissed her, his heat and scent engulfing her like the best security blanket ever invented.

He drove them south, two hours away from Whispering Springs, down a rutted road that required four-wheel drive and lots of hanging on. When they finally stopped, they were at a small, secluded cabin on the banks of a crystal clear lake. Chopped firewood was stacked in layers between two large trees. From her seat, Georgie could see a chimney, a couple of windows and that was about it.

"Tanner. It's so cute."

"Thanks. Belongs to an old buddy of mine. He doesn't get up here much but he says when he and his wife can, it's like being in their own little world."

When the word *wife* had left his lips, an electrical jolt went through her heart and her gut flipped.

"You okay?" he asked. "You look a little flushed."

"What? No, no. I'm fine. Let's take a look."

Cabin was the right word, but the place had a definite charm. The interior was completely constructed from split pine logs. A fairly modern kitchen, small dining area and a living room with an enormous fireplace made up the main area. There were two bedrooms, one smaller and one that was the obvious master with its king bed, and small fireplace. There was only one bathroom but it was spacious. The dining room had a set of french doors that led onto a deck that overlooked the lake. However, it was late enough in the evening for the lighting to be inadequate to fully appreciate the view.

Friday night was perfect. Dinner was hot dogs roasted over the flames from the fire Tanner had built in the living room fireplace. They made love in front of the fire after dinner, followed by a shower highlighted by more of a naked Tanner and then another round in the king bed. But not a word was said about their future. It tickled Georgie that he was stretching out the mystery.

If Friday night was perfect, Saturday was ideal. Early morning sunrays woke them for a long bout of lovemaking. Tanner went fishing behind the cabin while she sat on the deck and watched. She'd never get tired of looking at him. The view from every angle made her heart sigh. She laughed and clapped when he pulled in a couple of trout, which he cleaned for dinner.

That afternoon, a thunderstorm arrived bringing lightning and heavy rain. Trapped inside with rain pounding on the roof, a fire burning, and wrapped in Tanner's arms met every hot button Georgie had. Either then or later as they made love would have been an idyllic time for him to ask her. Still, nothing.

Sunday morning, hand-in-hand, they went for a walk along the lake. They talked about everything but nothing in particular. He did ask where she was going next. The question had sent her heart racing so fast it pumped all the blood from her heart and she got light-headed. When she explained she hadn't taken anything yet and she'd been thinking about taking a month or so off, he told her it was a great idea, even going so far as to suggest some great places for vacations. It took every acting skill she possessed to not laugh at his cute way of digging for information from her on where to take her on a honeymoon.

They made love before they left. It was slow and attentive, as though he were trying to touch and taste every inch of her skin. That would have been the perfect time for his proposal, but no. Nothing.

On the ride home, both of them were quiet. She couldn't think of anything left to say. She'd left it all behind at the cabin.

As they pulled behind the vet clinic so she could pick up her truck, he parked and turned off the engine. He turned in the seat toward her.

"This weekend was great."

This was it!

"I had a wonderful time. Thank you."

"Um…" He cleared his throat. "There is something I'd like to talk to you about."

"Yes," she blurted out. "I mean, sure. Fire away."

His brow furrowed. "I know we talked about this…this…well, whatever it is we have, ending when you leave."

"That's right." She straightened and leaned a little closer so she'd be available for his kiss.

"You're leaving on the twentieth, right?"

"Yes. A little under three weeks."

He combed his fingers through his hair, making it stand up in places. She didn't think he'd ever looked as cute as he did right now. This would be the story she would tell their children and their grandchildren. How nervous he was as he asked her to marry him. How he fidgeted and wouldn't meet her gaze.

She wondered if he had already bought her a ring as a surprise or if that was something they'd do together.

"Well," he drawled out. "I know we had an agreement, but I'm afraid I have to break my word."

Good Lord man. Spit it out. Didn't he realize that she was going to say yes?

"I've been offered Chief of the County Fire Department. Well Assistant Chief for now but Chief Townsend is retiring at the end of the year and the job is mine if I want it."

"Oh, Tanner. That's wonderful."

He shrugged and a slight flush colored his adorable cheeks. "It doesn't pay much, but I'd have time for a second job."

Wasn't he cute? He was worried about providing for them. Heck, she made enough, more than enough, for a second income.

"Maybe not," she said. "I mean, you just never know what's around the corner."

His face brightened. "That's true but that brings me back to us."

She leaned closer. "Yes?"

"I have to attend some advanced training courses at the National Fire Academy in Maryland. I'll be gone for the next three weeks. Those courses can get me ready for additional certifications that will be handy as Fire Chief. I was already a lieutenant with the Lexington Fire Department. I'm pretty stoked that the county is willing to financially support me in this. It's a heck of an opportunity."

His grin conveyed just how excited he was about these courses.

She frowned. Damn. She was going to have to lead the horse to the water.

"Okay. So how does this affect us?"

"Since I'll be up there so long, I'm driving to Maryland so I'll have my truck. I have to leave tomorrow night and I won't be back until a couple of days before Christmas." He shrugged, his smile gone from his beautiful mouth. "I hate that I won't be here to give you a proper goodbye. That's why I wanted this weekend for us. Something special that would give us the perfect way to end things. Don't you agree? I mean, we both knew it was coming. I just have to move it up and I felt awful about that."

She sat back, her face stinging as though she'd been slapped. "Oh."

Do not cry.

"I see. Well, this does catch me a little offguard."

Do not cry.

She swallowed against the solid stone in her throat.

He sighed and reached for her. "I know. I didn't want to say anything to spoil this weekend." He pulled her across the seat and into an embrace.

Her eyes were beginning to sting. She had to leave. *Do not cry.*

Georgie hugged him and then slid back across the truck and opened the door. "Good luck, Tanner. You'll be a great chief for the fire department." When she stood outside the truck, she leaned back in to say, "No need to get out. As you've pointed out, no reason to prolong the inevitable."

She grabbed her bag from the back seat, tossed it into the bed of her truck, climbed in, and drove away, all the while leaving Tanner sitting behind his steering wheel.

The minute she turned the corner out of Tanner's eyesight, the dam burst. Hot, salty tears poured down her face and dripped off her chin onto her shirt. Her chant changed from *do not cry* to *do not wreck*. It was like driving in a torrential downpour, except she didn't have adequate wipers for her eyes. Didn't matter what the speed limit, she tore home like the devil himself was behind her…but then, maybe he was.

Zack's truck was in her drive when she got home. She hastily wiped her face on the hem of her shirt and then ran her fingers through her hair. Before she got out, Zack was on her porch.

"Hey," he shouted. "You're home earlier than I thought you'd be. Why you sitting in there? Come on in. I'll get my stuff together to leave."

Georgie waited until his back was turned to exit. After retrieving her bag, she slowly walked up her stairs and into the house.

"Sorry," he shouted from the guest room. "I would have been long gone if I'd thought you'd be home at six but you know how it is with parents and siblings… any chance for some alone time."

"No," she replied. "Don't know how it is."

"Do what?" He popped his face around the door facing. "What'd you say? Ohmygod, Georgie. What's wrong?"

Zack hurried back to the living room where she stood, still holding her luggage in one hand.

"What happened?" he asked.

"Wh…what…makes…you…" she sniffed, "think…something…happened?" And the carefully reconstructed dam broke again. She dropped her luggage to the floor and covered her face.

"Oh man." Zack wrapped her in his arms. "What did my fool of a brother do?"

"He broke up with me," she cried.

"Do what? Are you kidding? Has he gone totally crazy?"

"I…I…don't know."

Zack patted her on the back. "He's an idiot. Really. A total idiot."

"It's okay," she said through tears, and continued sniffing. "We were going to end things anyway when I left, or that's what we said. He just caught me offguard tonight."

Zack held her away from him. "The two of you

had already planned a breakup? You had it sched-uled?" He shook his head in disbelief. "And I thought I was the screwed up one."

She chuckled and pushed away. "I just didn't think he'd do it like that." She walked to the open kitchen and began searching through cabinets.

He followed her. "Now what are you doing?"

Holding up a bottle of unopened bourbon, she said, "I'm gonna get drunk."

"It's not right for a lady to get drunk alone."

"You want a glass?" she asked as she filled a tumbler.

"Hit me."

She smiled and pulled a second glass down, which she filled. "Salute." She tapped her glass against his and shot the first drink down.

Closing her eyes, she allowed the fiery liquid to scald her throat as it rolled toward her stomach, where it landed with a splash. When she reopened her eyes he was watching her.

"I thought we were going to drink," she said.

He nodded and threw back his shot. "Damn. That's some fine whiskey."

"Hell, yeah. Only drink the best. I learned that from one of my foster dads." She picked up the bottle. "Let's adjourn to the living room. You can continue telling me what an ass your brother is."

They drank and talked for hours. Even in her inebriated state, Georgie knew there was no way Zack could drive home. When he fell asleep, or more actu-ally passed out, she stretched him out on the couch and covered him with a blanket. And then she staggered to her own bed.

On his back, feet crossed at his ankles, his arms behind his head, Tanner stared at his ceiling. The rock that'd formed in his gut made it impossible to eat dinner. The elephant sitting on his chest made breathing difficult. For a while, he wondered if he was having a heart attack. He was a little young for one for sure, but damn, he'd never hurt like this, not even when he fell off a ladder during training. He even considered driving to the hospital emergency room. In the end, he had to accept what his brain kept telling him…breaking it off with Georgina was the dumbest move he'd ever made.

Sure, they'd agreed on a limited time period to see each other. And maybe it did start off as something to bide his time and keep him sane while his parents were gone. But somewhere along the way, he'd fallen for her…lock, stock and barrel. Whether he could get over her wasn't even the issue. He didn't *want* to get over her. He wanted her back, with him, for as long as possible.

As that thought crawled through his head, he realized what he was telling himself…he had found the woman he wanted in his life for the rest of his life. He wanted to marry Georgina.

The big question was…did she want to marry him?

Had she fallen for him too? His first response was yes, of course she had, but that could be his ego speaking. Hell, it probably was his ego. He'd never had a girlfriend walk away from him like she'd done tonight.

If he was being honest, he'd thought she'd put up some argument about ending things so abruptly but no. She jumped in her truck and raced out of the lot as though on the starting line for the Daytona 500.

He sat upright. If he did not tell her how he felt and, instead, let her walk away, he'd never forgive himself. He'd always wonder *what if?*

The time reflected on his ceiling from his clock read four-thirty. He could be at her place by five and catch her before work. He had to tell her the truth before he left for Maryland.

Besides, she said she had some time off when she was done. She could stay here and they would be back together in no time.

After taking a quick shower and getting dressed, he stopped long enough in the kitchen to fill a travel mug with fresh coffee. Thank goodness for his mother and the automatic timer inventor for the coffee pot.

When he wheeled up to Georgina's house, he had to slam his brakes to keep from rear-ending Zack's truck. What the hell was Zack doing here?

Tanner flew from his truck up the front steps and pounded on the front door. "Zack!" he shouted. "Open this damn door." He continued to beat on the door and shout until his brother answered.

"What?"

Zack stood there in a pair of wrinkled sweat pants,

a T-shirt, no socks and a definite case of bedhead hair. He scratched his head. "What?" he asked, his eyes at half-mast.

Tanner shoved his way inside, red-hot rage pumping through his veins in place of blood. "What are you doing here? Where's Georgina?"

"Georgie? She's here. Probably still in bed." His brother had the audacity to yawn.

Grabbing his brother's T-shirt, Tanner jerked him toward him. "What the hell are you doing here? Did you sleep with my woman?"

"What is all the yelling?" Georgina came from her bedroom, still pulling on a long robe. "Tanner? What are you doing here?"

Instead of answering Georgina, Tanner shook his brother. "You knew Georgina was my gal."

"Look, asshole," Zack said with a sneer and jerking free from Tanner's hold. "You tossed her over. Can I help it if she would rather be with me?"

Tanner made a fist and slammed it upside his brother's face. Zack's head rocked back from the force. He stumbled backwards and then hit the floor.

"Tanner. What's wrong with you?" Georgina cried, hurrying over to where Zack lay sprawled on the floor. She dropped to her knees by his head. "Are you okay?" She touched the growing red spot on his face and then glared up at Tanner. "Have you lost your mind?"

A black hole developed in Tanner's chest where his heart used to reside. "Well, you wasted no time replacing me. What? You've got three weeks left so you figured fucking one Marshall is as good as another?"

Her eyes popped wide. "Excuse me?"

"You heard me."

Zack shook his head. "You have really fucked up this time, Tanner."

Tanner gave a snort of derision. "Yeah, I know. I showed up unexpectedly." He whirled on his boot heel. "I'll just leave you two lovebirds alone."

He slammed the front door so hard, the glass panes in the front windows rattled, not that he gave a shit. Hell, be fine with him if he broke one, or all, of them.

Throwing rocks and dirt, he whipped out of her drive and headed home. He wasn't waiting around for a gloating Zack to come home.

Within an hour of arriving back at the ranch, he had his truck packed and was ready to hit the road.

"Why wait?" he'd said to his parents. "I can get an early start and not have to drive at night."

His worthless, piece-of-shit brother was pulling up the drive as he was leaving. With all the maturity of a ten-year-old, Tanner gave Zack the finger and kept on going.

Fuck him.

And her too, now that he thought about it.

Pushing himself to get as far away from his treacherous brother and the duplicitous woman he'd fallen in love with, he'd driven Monday until his vision blurred and hallucinations appeared in his peripheral vision, only stopping long enough to nap in an interstate rest stop. He needed thousands of miles between himself and them.

How could they do this to him?

He loved Georgina. He loved his brother. But they had ripped his heart out and stomped on it. He wasn't sure he could ever go home again.

Chapter Twelve

Hell was not just a place preachers talked about on Sunday. Tanner was sure because he was in hell every day. Not the classes. Losing himself in the information and soaking up all he could about leadership, arson, and wild fire management were the only things that kept him sane. The nights were the worst. Sleep, when it came, was restless. Dreams of Zack and Georgina—nightmares really—where they laughed and pointed at him plagued him. A couple of times, a flash of auburn hair made him believe Georgina was there, but it never was her.

Damn, he missed her.

On the second week of classes, his phone rang. It was almost six in the evening. He'd only been home about fifteen minutes and had left his phone in a coat pocket. Now he ran across the room to answer.

"Hello?"

"Hi, honey. I hope I'm not interrupting your dinner," Janet Marshall said.

"Nope. Haven't started yet. Is something wrong?" He carried the phone to the small sofa in the hotel unit and sat.

"No, nothing's wrong. I just haven't talked to you in a few days. Your father and I wanted to make sure you were okay."

"Everything's fine."

"How are classes?"

"Good. Some of it's review, some of it's new."

"Well, that's good. We sure miss you here."

Yeah, he'd bet. Zack was probably gone all the time with Georgina and not pulling his fair share of work around the ranch.

"Are you sure everything's okay?"

"Have you talked to Zack?"

Zack, the traitor you mean?

"No. Why?"

"He's got a new girlfriend."

Tanner's heart squeezed and he lost his breath. "Oh? Anyone we know?"

He must be a glutton for punishment. Did he really want to hear her say Georgina's name?

"Not really," his mother said. "A townie named Delene."

"Delene? Delene Younger?"

"Yes, that's her. Do you know her?"

"Not well. Are you sure you got the name right?"

"Of course. He brought her to dinner this week. Seems like a nice girl."

"She is nice. I knew he'd been out with her a few times, but it's not like Zack to settle down with one girl."

"He's getting older and—oh, hold on. Here, say hi," his mother said.

He heard rattling as the phone receiver changed hands.

"Hello?"

The voice was a direct strike to his solar plexus, knocking the wind out of him.

"Georgina?"

"Yeah. How are classes?" Her voice could flash-freeze hot water.

"Good."

"Oh, good."

The conversation was awkward and stilted on both ends. He struggled for what to say.

"Here's your mom," Georgina said.

The rattle sounds reverberated again as the receiver changed hands.

"Thanks, Hon," his mother said to Georgina. "Okay. I'm back. The buzzer on my oven was going off."

"What is she doing there?"

"Who? Georgina? Having dinner with us."

"Is Jolene okay? Sir Henry?"

"Everybody's fine. Your sister did one of those shadow-someone assignments and Georgie was nice enough to let Deb hang onto her coattails for a day."

"I didn't mind," he heard Georgina say from the background.

"Still, it was nice of you," his mother replied, speaking to Georgina and not him. "Anyway, Deb enjoyed it so much, she shadowed Georgie for an entire weekend. And I thought having her over for dinner was the least your father and I could do as a thank you."

"It was nice of her," he agreed. "Can I speak to her for a second, unless you have something more to talk about with me?"

"Nope. I'm all done. Just making sure you're taking care of yourself. Hold on."

Rattle and then, "Yes?" *Brr.* Ice cold.

"I'm sorry about my brother."

"For what?"

"You know. Taking advantage of you and then just, well, walking away."

Her voice dropped to a quiet whisper. "You. Are. An. Idiot," she said, and hung up.

Poor Georgina. He knew his brother was too immature for a woman like Georgina and would have a million reasons why their night together "just happened." And that's why he'd not answered any of Zack's calls nor listened to any of his messages. He couldn't stomach hearing the excuses for Zack's behavior.

The sad thing was he did love his brother. The last thing he wanted to do was to spend the rest of his life feuding with Zack. They would just have to find a way to get past this.

A couple of days later when his phone rang, he

was driving in bright sunlight. Even if he'd tried, there was no way he could see the caller ID.

"Yeah?" Tanner answered.

"It's Zack."

Tanner gritted his teeth, fighting the rage that flared.

"Hold on. I'll pull over." Tanner turned into a shopping center parking lot and stopped his truck. "Okay. I'm here. Say your piece."

"Don't be a jackass, Tanner."

"You *want* me to hang up on you?"

"Hell, no. If you had listened to any of the fourteen million messages I left, nothing happened between me and Georgie. Nothing."

"Go on."

"Damn it, Tanner. Get this through your thick, jealous brain. Georgie was upset that you broke up with her. I had had an argument with…well, a woman I was seeing. We drank and talked until I fell asleep. Georgie threw a blanket over me and left. That's it. That's all that happened."

"Why didn't you tell me this when I walked in?"

"Maybe because you were too busy pounding my face. Hell, man. I was still a little drunk. And the cells that weren't booze-infused were hung over. You didn't give us time to explain. You hit me and marched out." Zack sighed. "You really hurt Georgie…bad."

His words dug deep into Tanner's soul.

"She didn't deserve what you did to her," Zack continued. "She loves you, or at least, she did love you.

Now? I wouldn't blame her if she wrote you off as a crazy person."

"You didn't have sex with Georgina?"

"How many times do I have to tell you? I. Did. Not. Have. Sex. With. Your. Girl. Georgie is a nice person, but she's too old for me."

Tanner had to smile at the last sentence. Hadn't he been saying the same thing? Maybe he had over-reacted.

"Sorry about your face."

Zack chuckled. "Not me. Got me loads of sympathy at Leo's, not to mention quite a few free beers."

Tanner sighed. "I am a fool."

"Yep. I have to agree."

"Thanks for your support," he replied with heavy sarcasm.

"You know you've got some serious groveling to do, don't you? I'm talking about you on your knees begging-for-forgiveness type of groveling. And that's if she doesn't slam the door in your face."

Tanner raked his fingers through his hair as he blew out a loud breath. "I still have another week up here."

"Well, bro, I'd suggest you think of how to do some nice stuff for her from afar. Good luck."

His phone calls to Georgina went unanswered that evening. Fine. He would apologize the old-fashioned way...cards and flowers. And pray that would soften her up.

"Make sure that Prissy gets two pills every day," Georgie said to Mrs. Willingham. "That will clear up that bladder infection."

Mrs. Willingham picked up her overweight and extremely spoiled Persian cat and cradled her. "Thank you, Dr. Greyson."

Georgie left the exam room and dragged her exhausted body down to her office to collapse on the sofa. She went to bed on time. She did every get-to-sleep-trick she knew or that she could find on the internet, but sleep continued to evade her. And when she did finally drift off, her dreams were always of Tanner walking out on her. Slamming the door. Damning her to a loveless life.

Every time she thought about that morning and Tanner's accusations she got mad all over again. After Chris left her to have an affair with her best friend, how could Tanner think that she would do the same?

She was in love with Tanner-the-idiot.

But give her a year, or ten, and she'd be okay again.

A rap on her door jerked her back to the present. "Dr. Greyson?"

"Come on in."

The clinic receptionist pushed the door open. "Look what came for you." She walked in carrying a dozen red roses arranged in a large white vase. Stems of baby's breath and greenery filled out the arrangement.

"Oh," Georgie said a little breathless. "It's beautiful. Set it on the desk." She stood and followed the receptionist to her desk so she could pull the envelope from the plastic stand shoved among the leaves.

The card inside read "Missing you."

No signature. No return address. But she suspected they were from Tanner, not that a bouquet of flowers could make up for what he said.

She dropped the card into the trash. "Take them to the front desk for our clients to enjoy."

The receptionist whipped around and carried them out.

Nope. She wouldn't be swayed by some red petals.

The next day, the office manager dropped off a couple pieces of mail for Georgie. One was a catalog of pet supplies and toys. The other was a blue envelope. Inside the blue envelope was a card.

The card cover was of a horse that looked surprisingly like Jolene. The inside had been left blank by the manufacturer but now had handwriting that read, "Saw this. Thought of you. Not surprising since I think of you every day."

Again no signature. She held the card over the trash can but her fingers would not let go. Finally, she opened her purse and shoved it inside to take home.

A day passed and nothing arrived, not that she expected to get something every day. That was nuts. Still, she left for home a little disappointed.

When she arrived home, an express delivery box was propped against her door. She picked it up and carried it into the house. She expected candy since he'd already sent flowers and a card. But she was wrong. The box was filled with greeting cards. Some made her laugh with the puns and jokes. But many of them were heartfelt declarations of love and loss. The largest one was heart-shaped. Inside Tanner had simply written:

> *I was wrong. I am sorry.*
> *I love you.*
> *Forgive me*
> *Tanner*

She dropped into a kitchen chair and read his message again.

He loved her.

She sort of suspected that he did. But that didn't solve their problems, did it? Her mind began firing memory pictures of their time together, the love they shared, the laughs, the quiet moments.

Her cell phone buzzed, pulling her from her thoughts.

She answered without looking at the screen. "Dr. Greyson."

A distinct crackle filled the air, followed by, "Georgie? It's James Mabee."

"James. What a nice surprise. Have you started home?"

"No, not yet. That's why I'm calling. My wife wants to stay another six weeks. Is that going to be a problem? Can you stay?"

"Of course I can stay."

"Great. Any problems at the clinic or at the house we found you?"

"Everything is going great. Love the house."

"Good. Good. Have you thought about settling in Whispering Springs? My wife and I are enjoying the travel and I need a partner. Love Dr. Brian but he can't handle as much as he used to."

"I…I…I hadn't thought about it."

Liar.

"Well, give it some thought. The guy that owns the house you're staying in has moved into an assisted living complex. The house with all the acreage will be going up for sale. If you decide to stay and are interested in the house, let me know and I'll get you in contact with him."

"Oh yes. I love the farm, and his pets he had to leave behind."

"Good. He'll be happy to know his animals won't have to be sold to strangers. Grab a pencil and let me give you the information."

He gave her the new contact information for the owner. Up to now, she'd been using direct draw to pay her rent, so she'd never contacted him. But she would now.

The second name and information was for his lawyer, KC Montgomery Gentry. His lawyer had his power of attorney and partnership papers should Georgie decide she wanted to settle in Whispering Springs.

After they hung up, she sagged against the back of

her chair, then she smiled. Then she burst out with laughter.

She thought about calling Tanner but didn't. He'd probably be happy to hear from her but she also didn't want for him to think a couple of cards and a bunch of flowers made up for the hurt he'd caused. He made this mess. She would let him clean it up. If she was going to spend the rest of her life with him—and she had every intention of doing so—then she wanted to let him come to her.

For the next week, she heard nothing from Tanner. No flowers, cards, or even text messages. She really wasn't good at romance. Maybe she was supposed to have called him after all the gifts. Argh. Someone hand her a rule book on dating and romance!

Friday night, she went to bed confused and sad. She had totally screwed up this thing with Tanner. Magda had told her to not call him and to stay tough and so she did. What was she doing taking advice from Magda, a woman who ran away the first time things got heavy with a guy?

A tapping at the door awoke her. Dawn was just breaking. Orange and purple streaks painted the sky.

She sat up and listened. There it was again. Someone was knocking at her back door.

Putting on a robe, she stumbled through the kitchen and peeked out the window before she answered.

Tanner stood there. A lightning bolt of lust, desire and love stunned her as it vibrated her body. Dressed in jeans, a flannel shirt, boots and a heavy coat, he'd never looked better.

"Tanner?"

"Don't ask questions. Just get dressed. I want to take you somewhere."

"What?"

"Get dressed." He leaned in and kissed her. "Trust me. Dress warm. Hurry."

"But…"

He put his hands on her shoulders, turned her around, and pushed her toward her bedroom.

"Warm clothes." He nuzzled behind her ear. "Please."

She hurried off to throw on jeans, a blouse, heavy sweater, boots and a jacket. As a last minute thought, she grabbed gloves and a hat. The breeze through the door had been quite nippy.

Once in his truck, they didn't drive far, only about a mile. In the open field stood a hot air balloon.

"Are you serious?" she asked.

"Yep. Come on."

Tanner climbed out and raced around to her side, lifting her out of his truck and onto the ground. They went through a gate and trudged through the dead grass to where five people held the balloon tethered to the ground.

"Climb in," Tanner said.

She looked at him, hesitated, and then nodded. If their future was to be together, she had to learn to trust him. In her heart, Georgie knew Tanner would never deliberately do anything that would hurt her.

He followed her into the basket, introduced her to the pilot, Jim, and then the guys holding the ropes released them. They floated off the ground in a quiet lift-off. The earth fell away. The only sound was the occasional blast of gas and flame to heat the air in the balloon to keep them aloft.

She stood looking out over the countryside. Being December, the fields were asleep for winter but they still provided homes for the cows and horses in the area. They were low enough that the animals would look up as they floated over.

"This is incredible, Tanner. I've never done this before."

He put his arms around her and pulled her back snug against his chest. "Let me tell you why I brought you up here."

"Okay."

"When I'm with you, this is how I feel. I'm floating. The chaos of the world is gone. My mind is quiet. My heart is light. I'm at peace. Only you do this for me. I'd be lying if I told you I'd never told a woman that I loved her. I have. But it's always been a lie, until now. I've never felt for a woman the way I feel for you. You make me look beyond just the field where I'm standing." He swept his arm out in front of her. "You make me see everything. Make me believe I can do anything. I love you, Georgina Greyson with all my heart."

Georgie looked over her shoulder. "That was beautiful."

"Wait. I have to say more. I am so sorry for all the

stupid things I said. I know you would never be unfaithful. Now, my brother…?"

She chuckled. "Nothing happened."

"I know. I think I knew it when I calmed down but by then, my foot was so far down my throat I was choking on it. Can you forgive me?"

"It might take me a long time."

"Like the rest of your life?"

"Yeah. That would be a start."

He turned her around so they were facing each other and dropped to one knee. "I love you, Georgina. I want to spend the rest of my life spoiling you. Will you marry me?"

Looking down, Georgina knew her future was bright.

"You drive me crazy, Tanner Marshall."

He grinned. "Is that a yes?"

She smiled. "That's a yes. I'll marry you."

He stood and enfolded her in his arms for a kiss.

"Hold on," the pilot said. "We're landing and it's a little rougher than the take off."

Georgie settled into Tanner's protective embrace as the pilot released the hot air and they slowly began to fall back down to earth. She was enough of a realist to know sometimes life would toss them a rough landing every now and then, but with Tanner as her co-pilot, she was ready to hit the ground running. Their life together was going to be an adventure, and she couldn't wait for it to begin.

New York Times and USA Today Bestselling Author Cynthia D'Alba was born and raised in a small Arkansas town. After being gone for a number of years, she's thrilled to be making her home back in Arkansas living on the banks of an eight-thousand acre lake.

Photo by Tom Smarch

When she's not reading or writing or plotting, she's doorman for her spoiled border collie, cook, housekeeper and chief bottle washer for her husband and slave to a noisy, messy parrot. She loves to chat online with friends and fans.

Send snail mail to: Cynthia D'Alba PO Box 2116 Hot Springs, AR 71914

Or better yet! She would for you to take her news-letter. She promises not to spam you, not to fill your inbox with advertising, and not to sell your name and email address to anyone. Check her website for a link to her newsletter.

www.cynthiadalba.com
cynthiadalba@gmail.com

Read on for more
Whispering Springs, Texas books
by
Cynthia D'Alba

TEXAS TWO STEP

WHISPERING SPRINGS, TEXAS BOOK 1 ©2012
CYNTHIA D'ALBA

Secrets are little time-bombs just waiting to explode.

After six years and too much self-recrimination, rancher Mitch Landry admits he was wrong. He left Olivia Montgomery. Now he'll do whatever it take to convince Olivia to give him a second chance.

Olivia Montgomery survived the break-up with the love of her life. She's rebuilt her life around her business and the son she loves more than life itself. She's not proud of the mistakes she's made—particularly the secret she's kept—but when life serves up manure, you use it to mold yourself into something better.

At a hot, muggy Dallas wedding, they reconnect, and now she's left trying to protect the secret she's held on to for all these years.

Read on for an excerpt:

The woman stood on tiptoe in the baggage-claim area of the Dallas/Fort Worth airport looking for all the world like someone who'd been sent to collect the devil. Mitch Landry had expected Wes or one of the other groomsmen to come for him. Instead, his gaze found a statuesque blonde arching up on her toes, a white T-shirt with Jim's Gym in black script stretched across her lushly curved breasts and long tanned legs extending from tight denim shorts. His heart stumbled then roared into a gallop.

Blood rushed from his brain to below his waist. His nostrils flared in a deep breath, as though he could smell her unique fragrance across the crowded lobby.

She hadn't looked in his direction yet, which gave him an unfettered opportunity to study her without having to camouflage his reactions.

No make-up covered her creamy rose complexion, not that she needed any. Not then and not now. No eye shadow was required to bring out the deep blue of her eyes. Nor did her mouth need any enhancement. Her lips radiated a natural pink, although the bottom one grew redder as her upper teeth gnawed on it.

Six years had passed since he'd seen Olivia Montgomery, but he'd swear she was more beautiful today. She had an appeal that came only with age and maturity. A smile edged onto his mouth. He was surprised —pleasantly surprised—to admit how glad he was to see her.

He watched as her glare bounced around the room, searching faces until it fell on him. As a look of resignation flashed across her face, she frowned.

His smile faded. Not exactly the reaction he'd hoped for.

TEXAS TANGO

WHISPERING SPRINGS, TEXAS, BOOK 2 © 2013
CYNTHIA D'ALBA

Sex in a faux marriage can make things oh so real.

Dr. Caroline Graham is happy with her nomadic lifestyle fulfilling short-term medical contracts. No emotional commitments, no disappointments. She's always the one to walk away, never the one left behind. But now her grandmother is on her deathbed, more concerned about Caroline's lack of a husband than her own demise. What's the harm in a little white lie? If a wedding will give her grandmother peace, then a wedding she shall have.

Widower Travis Montgomery devotes his days to building the ranch he and his late wife planned before he lost her to breast cancer. The last piece of acreage he needs is controlled by a lady with a pesky need of her own. Do her a favor and he can have the land. She needs a quick, temporary, faux marriage in exchange for the acreage.

It's a total win-win situation until events begin to snowball and they find, instead of playacting, they've put their hearts at risk.

Read on for an excerpt:

Friday afternoon, Travis Montgomery pulled his truck under the only shade tree in the Montgomery and Montgomery Law Offices parking lot. He hoped his brother had some news for him about Fitzgerald's place. After ten years of unsuccessfully trying to get Old Man Fitzgerald to sell, Singing Springs Ranch would finally be his. He could feel it in his bones.

He hadn't known Fitzgerald had family, so finding out Caroline Graham was his great-niece was a tad of a surprise, but no big deal. Other than Caroline, no other Fitzgerald family members mentioned in the obit lived here. He couldn't imagine that old tightwad leaving his ranch to any of them. And even if he did, there was no way anyone would up and move to Texas just because they inherited a rundown ranch, especially if that person knew nothing about ranching. Yup. Whoever ended up with Singing Springs would be thrilled to unload it, and Travis wanted to make sure that person unloaded it right into his hands.

He let himself in the back door of his brother's office, stopping long enough to grab a bottle of cold water from the kitchen, then headed for the reception area.

After removing his beige straw cowboy hat, he leaned over the reception desk to give Jason's secretary a wink. "Hi, Mags. Is little brother available?"

"Hey, handsome," Margaret said then sighed. "If only I were twenty years younger and not married…"

Travis slapped his hat across his heart. "My bachelor days would be over."

She smiled and nodded toward the closed door

down the hall. "He's on the phone. I'll let him know you're here. I'd offer you something to drink, but you seemed to have helped yourself."

He rolled the dewy bottle on the back of his neck. "Can't decide if I want to drink this or pour it over my head. Man, it's a killer out there. What about KC? Is my lovely cousin around?"

Before Margaret could respond, Jason's door opened. "I thought I heard a reprobate out here. Stop flirting with my secretary and c'mon back. I've got a date with Lydia tonight and you know she hates when I'm late." He ducked back into his office, leaving the door ajar.

Travis groaned. "I'm coming." He looked at Margaret and hitched his thumb toward the door where his brother had just been standing. "He been in this bad mood all day?"

She shook her head. "Nope. He was quite pleasant when KC headed out about thirty minutes ago. Your cousin's got perfect timing. She always knows to clear out and avoid the Montgomery brothers when something's brewing."

"Lucky me. Wish I knew her magic."

Travis entered his brother's office and closed the door behind him. He dropped onto the thick leather sofa running along the office wall then set his hat crown-side down on the cushion beside him. He draped his arm along the back of the sofa. "I hope you've got some good news for me. I've had a bitch of a day."

"What happened?"

"One of the Webster kids spooked a new stallion I'd just unloaded. The bastard almost trampled me, John and a couple of hands before we could get him under control."

Jason frowned. "I'd think your foreman's kids would know better than to get near a stallion, especially one I suspect was antsy to begin with. Which kid?"

Travis's mouth cocked up on one side in a grimace. "Rocky. He had a classmate visiting, and I think he was trying to impress him. But after John and Nadine get done with him, I suspect his ears will be ringing for the next week." He gave a small chuckle. "And I'm getting my stalls mucked out for free for at least a month, maybe two."

"I hated mucking stalls."

"So I remember. What's the good news?"

Jason took a seat closer to the sofa. "Well, I've got good news and bad news."

"Great. Bad news first then."

"Fitzgerald had KC prepare his will about a year ago, so his estate won't be going to the state to resolve."

Travis scowled. "I was afraid of that," he growled. "So what can you tell me now?"

"All the beneficiaries have been notified and the will duly probated. It was fairly straight forward. I don't foresee anyone challenging it."

"So don't keep me waiting. Who do I need to talk to about buying Singing Springs?"

"Dr. Caroline Graham."

TEXAS FANDANGO

WHISPERING SPRINGS, TEXAS BOOK 3 © 2014
CYNTHIA D'ALBA

Two-weeks on the beach can deepened more than tans.

Attorney KC Montgomery has loved family friend Drake Gentry ever since they were kids, but she never seemed to be on his radar. Fate puts in the same bar when Drake's girlfriend dumps him, leaving him with two all-expenses paid tickets to the Sand Castle Resort in the Caribbean. KC seizes the chance and makes him an offer impossible to refuse: two weeks of food, fun, sand, and sex with no strings attached.

University Professor Drake Gentry has noticed his best friend's cousin for years, but KC has always been hands-off, until today. Unable to resist, he agrees to her two-week, no-strings affair.

The vacation more than fulfills both their fantasies. The sun is hot but the sex hotter. Once home, KC finds it harder than she had expected to go back to her regular life. For Drake, their short two-week fling leaves him wanting more, but what's he to do when KC makes it clear she wants nothing more?

TEXAS TWIST

WHISPERING SPRINGS, TEXAS BOOK 4 © 2014
CYNTHIA D'ALBA

Real bad boys can grow up to be real good men.

Paige Ryan lost everything important in her life. She moves to Whispering Springs, Texas to be near her step-brother. But just as her life is starting to get back on track, it's derailed again when the last man in the world she wants to see again moves into her house.

Cash Montgomery is on the cusp of having it all. But a bad bull ride leaves him injured and angry. His only comfort is found at the bottom of a bottle. His family drags him home to Whispering Springs, Texas, the last place he wants to be. With nowhere to go, he moves temporarily into an old ranch house on his brother's property surprised the place is occupied.

The best idea is to move on but sometimes taking the first step out the door is the hardest one.

Loving a bull rider is dangerous, so is falling for him a second time is crazy?

TEXAS BOSSA NOVA

WHISPERING SPRINGS, TEXAS BOOK 5 ©2014
CYNTHIA D'ALBA

A heavy snowstorm can produce a lot of heat

Magda Hobbs loves being a ranch housekeeper. The job keeps her close to her recently discovered father, foreman at the same ranch. She is immune to all the cowboy charms, except for one certain cowboy, who is wreaking havoc on her libido.

Reno Montgomery is determined to make his fledgling cattle ranch a success. He's content with the occasional date until Magda Hobbs. She is rocking his world and then she's gone, leaving him confused and more than a little angry. He's shocked when he learns the new live-in housekeeper is Magda Hobbs.

When a freak snowstorm cuts off the outside world, the isolation rekindles their desire. But when the weather and the roads clear, Reno has to work hard and fast to keep the woman of his dreams from hitting the road right out of his life again.

TEXAS HUSTLE

WHISPERING SPRINGS, TEXAS BOOK 6 ©2015
CYNTHIA D'ALBA

Watch out for chigger bites, love bites and secrets that bite

Born into a wealthy, Southern family, Porchia Summers builds a good life in Texas until a bad news ex-boyfriend tracks her down. Desperate for time to figure out how to handle the trouble he brings, she looks to the one man who can get her out of town for a few days.

Darren Montgomery has had his eye on the town's sexy, sweet baker for a while but she's never returns his looks until now. He's flattered but suspicious about her quick change in attention.

Sometimes, camping isn't just camping. It's survival.

TEXAS LULLABY

WHISPERING SPRINGS, TEXAS BOOK 7 ©2016
CYNTHIA D'ALBA

Sometimes what you think you don't want is exactly what you need.

After a long four-year engagement, Lydia Henson makes her decision. Forced to choice between having a family or marrying a man who adamantly against fathering children, she chooses the man. She can live without children. She can't live without the man she loves.

Jason Montgomery doesn't want a family, or at least that's his story and he's sticking to it. The falsehood is less emasculating than the truth.

On the eve of their wedding, Jason and Lydia's well-planned life is thrown into chaos. Everything Jason has sworn he doesn't want is within his grasp. But as he reaches for the golden ring, life delivers another twist.

TEXAS DAZE

WHISPERING SPRINGS, TEXAS BOOK 9 ©2017
CYNTHIA D'ALBA

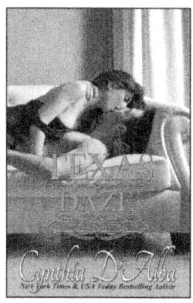

A quick fling can sure heat up a cowgirl's life

When a devastating discovery ends Marti Jenkins' engagement, she decides to play the field for a while. A ranch accident lands her in the office of Whispering Springs' new orthopedic doctor, Dr. Eli Boone. And yeah, he's as hot as she's been told.

Dr. Eli Boone is temporarily covering his friend's practice and then it's back to New York City and the societal world he's lives. He's not looking for a wife, but he wouldn't say no to a quick tumble in the sheets with the right woman.

Due to ridiculous challenge, Eli has to learn to ride before he leaves town. He turns to the one person who can help him win the bet, Marti Jenkins.

As he learns to ride a horse, Marti does a little riding of her own…and she doesn't need a horse.

Printed in Great Britain
by Amazon